TRANQ

JAINA SANGA grew up in Bombay and moved to the US in 1980 as a student. After receiving a PhD in English from Case Western Reserve University in Cleveland, she taught English and Cultural Studies for several years. She is the author of a critical book on Salman Rushdie's fiction and editor of two volumes on South Asian literature. Her short stories have appeared in a number of literary journals. *Silk Fish Opium* is her first novel. She lives in Dallas and travels to India frequently.

SILK FISH OPIUM

Jaina Sanga

Jaina Sanga (signature)

TRANQUEBAR

TRANQUEBAR PRESS
An imprint of westland ltd
Venkat Towers, 165, P.H. Road, Opp. Maduravoyal Municipal office, Chennai 600 095
No. 38/10 (New No.5), Raghava Nagar, New Timber Yard Layout, Bangalore 560 026
23/181, Anand Nagar, Nehru Road, Santacruz East, Mumbai 400 055
4322/3, Ansari Road, Daryaganj, New Delhi 110 002

First published in India in TRANQUEBAR PRESS by westland ltd 2012

Copyright © Jaina Sanga 2012

10 9 8 7 6 5 4 3 2 1

ISBN: 978-93-81626-83-2

Typeset in 11/14 pts. Adobe Jenson Pro by SÜRYA, New Delhi
Printed at Thomson Press

The copyright for W.H. Auden's 'Partition' (*Collected Poems*, Faber & Faber, 2007) rests
with Curtis Brown Ltd, NY. All efforts have been made to contact the copyright holders
for permission.

For my father,
Max.

You phoned every day to ask about the novel.
Wish you could see this.

Contents

Prologue

An orange glow, a whiff of smoke, and the flames came to life, seething and spreading from the head down the tiny recumbent body. Motilal stared at the fire, at once amazed and horrified at how the flames consumed what was once living flesh, until he had to look away, to the betel palms at the far side of the cremation ground where a man was stacking wood, appraising each log before setting it down. Motilal's eyes wandered to the ebbing tide, as if the sea could tell him how he had lost his daughter. For what cruel deed in a past life was he atoning? He wanted to wrench himself from this place and from this existence, give himself to the waves and float away on their frothy crests. But he was there, on the grey beach, his legs heavy and awkward as the bolts of silk that filled his godown. There would be no floating away on the waves. He dug his calloused heels into the sand, blackened with ash, bristly between his toes, and returned his attention to the pyre.

Next to Motilal, the other men – his sons, nephews, neighbours, and brother – all dressed in white, were solemnly watching the fire. At his wife's insistence, he'd sent for the barber early in the morning and he and his two sons had had their heads tonsured. He could hardly recognize his sons . . . how old and grim they appeared in their baldness.

Motilal had attended many cremations; two he remembered, vividly. When his father died there were crowds at the ghats near the river. It was raining, a torrential downpour, clattering on the tin roof that barely covered the pyre. His older brother held an umbrella and kept staring at the ground; the task of lighting the pyre fell to Motilal. He could see clearly the thin, tall boy of fourteen that he was recite the prayers as instructed and place the kindling on his father's head, light the thin strands of white hair and watch with fascination as the fire consumed the body until, an hour or so later, all that was left was pumice and ash – an entire lifetime reduced to powdery debris. It hadn't seemed real to him, but he understood that it was natural and rational. The ancient Vedas proclaimed that birth and death were merely aspects of life's cosmic cycle, and this he believed to be true.

The death of his first wife, Vasanta, many years later, had shaken him, drained him, unsettled him even now. It was the image of her lying in bed – cold cloths on her fevered neck and forehead – that came to him. The chloroquine had worked initially and the doctor said her malaria was abating – Motilal even went to the office that afternoon, stopping on the way at the temple to give thanks and far too much money – but the next day the fever returned. More medicine, he urged the doctor, and then he was screaming: 'Do something!' The doctor shook his head, put away his stethoscope and slipped out of the room. Motilal sat with her limp, defeated form until someone came with basin and cloth to wash the body. In the months that followed, Motilal's world was dark until, unexpectedly, a temporary exuberance for life returned and he married Harshaba.

At the cremations of his father and his first wife, the flames had given off occasional popping sounds. It's the fat and muscle burning, someone whispered to him. He was ready now for those morbid little explosions from the fire. But there were none; only smoke and flames and the wood turning to glowing charcoal underneath. He absently scratched at his neck where a mosquito bite had swelled into a red welt.

ౚౚ

In the main hall of his house the women had cried softly as they sprinkled marigolds on the shroud covering the bamboo bier. The bier in turn had been placed under the big chandelier. The *pujari*, a diminutive man with sparse white hair, loose brown skin and droopy cheeks, led the chants in a plaintive, ceremonious voice, the words amplified by the walls of the high marble walls of the *divankhana*. After the prayers, the house servants, gardeners and cooks were called to pay their last respects. They shuffled around the bier in single file, their heads lowered, some looking confused and others sincerely sad. Vincent, the driver, who was a Christian, had dressed in a black suit he had borrowed from a schoolteacher in the fishing village. He stood to the side, watching the Hindu ritual. Approaching the bier, he burst out angrily, 'I don't believe this! What has come over you?' He gestured wildly at Motilal and Harshaba. Someone pulled him away, hurried him outside.

Four men hoisted the bier onto their shoulders and some thirty men fell in behind them. The women had no place at the cremation and waited at the house. Outside, a few rays of sunlight pierced the dawn, a hazy half-moon began fading in the northeast. As the *chowkidars* opened the compound gates, a line of crows, squabbling on the rooftop, launched noisily into the sky. Someone gasped and whispered that it was a bad omen; the ancestors were annoyed.

ೞ

The fire smelled faintly sweet. The pujari's assistants had placed sandalwood and sticks of incense between the folds of cloth on the bier. Motilal inhaled and the aroma took him to an attar shop near his office on Muhammad Ali Road, and he thought he was there, dousing himself with strong perfumes. He didn't want to leave that shop.

As Motilal watched the chanting pujari toss rice and ghee into the flames he could feel the heat from the fire on his face. Sweat trickled down his neck; his soaked *kurta* clung to his chest. Death was not easy for the living, he pondered – the eleven-day mourning period would begin tomorrow, and relatives dressed in white would sweep through the house offering condolences while sniggering behind his back. In time they would forget, he hoped. He shut his eyes against a light wind that whirled the smoke in his direction. His throat was dry and he wanted a bath.

So many things to do. Someone would have to go to Haridwar or Banaras to immerse the ashes in the Ganges. The time he had gone with his brother and their father's ashes, they had recited the final prayers on the dhow and lowered the copper urn in the water. Inside the urn were gold rings and silver coins, last offerings to the departed soul. Behind them, from a rowboat, a scrawny boy jumped into the water and chased the urn as it drifted downriver. His accomplice in the rowboat rowed hard to keep up. The young scavengers were poor Muslim boys for whom the Ganges held no spiritual significance. From the dhow, Motilal's brother yelled at the boy to leave their father's urn alone. The boy waved, flashed a smile and then his glistening, brown, wiry arms kept stroking against the current. When he ducked under water, Motilal held his breath and watched silently. He wanted the boy to find the urn, to win the gold ring and silver coin. The sediment of the Ganges was rich enough and life was for the living. After four or five attempts, the boy surfaced clutching something under one arm and swam sidestroke, upriver, towards the rowboat. Motilal smiled and thought his father would have approved. His brother looked sour. It was a long ago memory, but he could almost hear now beyond the beach the boys cheering their success.

Now at the cremation ground the fire finally faded. The wind that had earlier fanned its flames made short work of the last of its fuel. The pujari's assistants began directing everyone to leave as they collected the ash.

Motilal's eyes skipped from face to face. His eldest son, Shrikant, nodded and shrugged his shoulders. Motilal didn't understand the gesture and kept looking at him, but Shrikant turned away. Mahesh, his second son, held Motilal's gaze, looked him straight in the eye. The corners of Mahesh's mouth creased. It wasn't quite a smile, but a look of pity that comprehended his father's predicament. Motilal turned, plunged his hands into his pockets, and stared at the ground.

At the gates to the cremation area, a lorry decorated with banners and flags cruised past, forcing them to the side of the road. Raucous music spilled out of the driver's side window. Behind the lorry several raggedly dressed children pranced about, some of them trying to grab hold of the vehicle and pull themselves aboard. A man in a white kurta, white *topi* angled on his head, brushed at the children with one hand while holding a megaphone in his other. He raised the megaphone to his mouth. 'We got rid of the British, now we must get rid of socialist bigots, we must get rid of Congress bigots. We must make a new India.'

Motilal stared after the truck, his eyes intent on the man whose black-framed glasses reminded him of Subhas Chandra Bose, India's forgotten ambassador of freedom. Bose had scoffed at Gandhi's tactics of non-violence against the British Raj – 'Give me blood and I will get you freedom,' was Bose's motto. But Bose was killed in a plane crash two years ago.

The voice over the megaphone continued: 'We must make a new India . . . make a new India . . . a new India.'

The phrase rang in the crowded street as the lorry was swallowed by the city and, Motilal, left with the sadness of his daughter's death, hurried to catch up with the other men.

I
HARMONIUM

Chapter 1

As the *chuum-chuum* jingle of anklets marked the three tall steps to the stage, Hanif glanced up from the harmonium and caught a flutter of the girl's bright pink sari, startling against the blue velvet curtains. He nodded at the slight smile she sent as apology in his direction and continued playing. He was the senior student assistant, in the final year of his BA, enlisted by the music department to coach the first and second years; it made no difference to him whether they came on time or not. She was probably new – he did not recognize her – and as confused as he often still was by the meandering corridors of the college. He looked up again. The fingers of his right hand drifted off the keyboard, his left hand stopped pumping the bellows, and the music waned. The singers were left in mid-range; a few stray voices sang a phrase or two before petering out. Chuum-chuum, *chamak-chamak* – she hurried across the stage.

A train rumbled nearby into Bombay's Victoria Station. From the road below the auditorium came the honks of cars and taxis, the groan of a bus leaving the college stop. A few pigeons fluttered into the overgrown tamarind tree outside the window closest to the stage. The wobbly ceiling fans, at full speed, lifted the pages of an old music book that lay open next to Hanif's harmonium.

Hanif tried not to stare at the girl as she found her place in the second row among the others sitting cross-legged on the stage floor. He noticed the drape of her sari, the way it hinted at the curve of her hips, her colourful bangles, the flower pinned in her braided hair, and the graceful way she lowered herself to the bare stage; no one moved to make space for her on the *dhurrie* and he flinched a little at her discomfort.

His fingers found the keyboard again. '*Chalo, ruk kyon gaye?* Come on, why have you stopped?' he reprimanded them, and began singing the *raga* himself. Taking his cue, and with a few voices trailing, the session resumed. The girl's face relaxed as she sang. Hanif played the harmonium louder and faster, with such gusto that several of the singers raised their eyebrows at each other.

At the end of the session, Hanif packed up the harmonium. He closed the bellows without draining the excess air and threw the cotton cover haphazardly over the instrument. Amid the general commotion of the dispersing class, he watched the girl leave – chuum-chuum, chamak-chamak.

ನಿ

At twenty-one, Hanif was one of the best up-and-coming musicians in Bombay, perhaps the next Mukesh Kumar or Muhammad Rafi. Usually he was humming or thinking of lines to a *ghazal*, but now as he walked to the station with his book bag slung over his shoulder, he was quiet. Around him, on the crowded footpaths, *bhaji-wallas* had already started setting up for the evening bazaar – pyramids of tomatoes, cabbages, turnips, bunches of cilantro and spinach, baskets laden with green and red chillies. With bare hands, the bhaji-wallas flicked liberal amounts of water on the produce to keep it fresh. A few droplets landed on Hanif's sandalled feet.

Pervez waved and shouted from across the road. Dodging an over-eager *tonga* on the lookout for passengers, he made his way towards Hanif and they continued to the station together. Compared to Hanif, Pervez was small-boned and thin; his pale skin and distinctive manner of speech conveyed his Parsi origins. He was a year younger than Hanif, and after sitting next to each other at a college assembly they'd become friends.

'Gandhiji is coming to Bombay next week,' Pervez said. 'He's giving a speech at the High Court grounds. Want to go?'

Hanif shifted his bag to the other shoulder and craned his neck.

'Who are you looking for?' Pervez asked. 'And why are you walking so fast?'

Hanif leaned towards Pervez, 'That girl up ahead . . .'

'Which girl? Are you asking about Rohini? Rohini Chimanji?'

'Rohini . . .'

'You're a senior, and you're asking about a first year?'

'She's in my music group. That's all.' Hanif watched the girl for several seconds more before she became a part of the sea of commuters near the station gate.

At the cold-drink kiosk on the platform, Hanif and Pervez stood drinking *falooda* while waiting for the train.

'Here, read this,' Pervez said, handing Hanif a smudgy

cyclostyle leaflet. 'See, Gandhi and Churchill will never come to an agreement. Churchill doesn't understand the civil disobedience campaign. Churchill doesn't understand Gandhiji. He called him a mediocre, half-naked lawyer the first time they met, and his view hasn't changed in nearly twenty years . . .'

Hanif stuffed the leaflet in a side pocket of his bag and rubbed absently at the ink it had left on his hands. Rohini. He repeated the name to himself. *Rohini. Rohini.* He tested the syllables, trying to decide which would sound better in a song.

'. . . Churchill wants a civil war between Hindus and Muslims. Nothing would please him more. During the Bengal famine, he said he didn't care about the food shortage in India. Can you believe that? He doesn't think India is capable of self-rule; he said we're a country of barbarians. Gandhi and Nehru are trying their best to negotiate.'

'Nothing's going to happen,' Hanif said. 'The Raj has been around for two hundred years. My father says the British are getting rich here. Giving up India would spell the doom of Lancashire.'

ನಞ

Hanif lived with his parents in a modest one-storey house, the once white exterior weathered and grey from many monsoons. His mother had tried to grow roses in the front garden, then sunflowers, but the shadow of the neighbour's banyan tree prevented all but the toughest patches of grass from surviving.

The music room at the back of the house was bright and airy, with two big windows facing the morning sun. There was a wooden chest filled with songbooks, a pair of old upholstered chairs, a table with an ancient hulking radio set, and another larger table with the newer, smaller radio and the record player, beside which were two neat stacks of jacketed vinyl records, one of smaller forty-fives and the other of thirty-threes, protected from dust under frayed lacy white cloths. An oval mirror hung on the west-facing wall next to a framed print of the Kaaba at Mecca.

Abbu, Hanif's father, worked in an accounting firm and wanted Hanif to become a barrister or an engineer, but he didn't interfere when he saw how passionate his son was about music. Ammi, his mother, encouraged his interest. She came from a family of musicians and she herself had been a classical dancer. Her ancestors, she proudly believed, had performed in Emperor Jehangir's court. It was Ammi's father who had given them his harmonium. At eighty-six, when his arthritic fingers refused to straighten, he decided that his youngest grandson, Hanif, who was barely crawling at the time, had music in his veins; he had noticed, he said, how the boy stopped crying whenever a song played on the radio.

The harmonium had its own place, on a small red carpet in the centre of the music room. When Hanif was four years old, Ammi made inquiries at their mosque for a music teacher and she was told about the blind man, who took Hanif on 'for the pleasure of hearing him learn to make music' and taught him a ghazal written by the Moghul Emperor, Bahadur Shah. The verses described the old, withered emperor, exiled and incarcerated by the British in Burma, yearning for his once great kingdom in India. During Ramadan, Ammi dressed little Hanif in a blue silk kurta and turban, and he sang the ghazal for the fifty or so family members and friends who had crammed into the house. Everyone cheered. '*Wah! Wah! Subhan'allah!*' said his father and uncles, gesturing to heaven with their palms. His mother, who thought he looked like a young emperor, said to the other women, 'We have our own Bahadur.' The comment filled Hanif with pride. At every Ramadan, and every Eid, after the prayers and feasting, it was understood that Hanif would perform. Over the years, he learned dozens of ghazals, and always, when they asked for an encore, he sang the one about Bahadur Shah.

Chapter 2

At fifty-seven, Rohini's father, Motilal, had the early signs of a protruding belly. His skin, several shades lighter than that of most Indians, his wide, distinctive forehead, and his straight, noble nose provided the prototype for two generations of the family. He was considered a handsome man, a trait that took on a degree of sophistication in sepia photos and oil portraits that he would commission photographers and artists to make twenty years later. Although he had no formal education to speak of – he'd studied only up to the third standard in a Gujarati medium school – he ran and expanded the silk business inherited from his father.

Rohini was his daughter by his second wife, Harshaba; his first wife had died a few weeks after giving birth to a son and Harshaba had embraced the boy as her own. Harshaba was a small woman with prematurely grey hair, large expressive eyes, and a flat nose on which she wore a glamorous *nathni*. By the time Rohini – her third child – was born, the demure expression of Harshaba's face had given in to age, which she made no attempt at hiding; the timbre of her voice had gone from mellow and gentle to stern and determined, tinged with frustration.

Motilal and Harshaba, along with their six children ranging in age from infant to twenty-three, had moved south from Ahmedabad to Bombay in the 1930s, and settled with all their belongings – old mattresses, even older kitchen utensils, odd pieces of furniture, and piles of second-hand clothes – at Kanji Mansion on Sandhurst Road. Hardly a mansion, the building comprised shabby, crowded flats, where the goings-on in one household became common knowledge in a matter of minutes.

Three years after moving to Bombay, Motilal's silk business reaped unprecedented profits; Laxmi, goddess of wealth, to whom he prayed once in a while, finally got around to him, he would often later say, and he built a house for his family on the outskirts of the city, at a place called Versova.

He named the house, Sagar Mahal – in English, Sea Palace. It sat majestically on a sandy beach with the vast expanse of the Arabian Sea as a luminous backdrop. Even from the road, behind the imposing green iron gates and the latticed compound wall, the house appeared stately. Wide verandahs encircled it and gardens with fountains and lotuses stretched out on either side. Every year, after the monsoons, Motilal hired a team of painters to give the house a fresh coat of yellow.

Rohini was five years old when the family moved from the cramped flat on Sandhurst Road to the grand house at Versova. During those early days a red public bus made three trips a day from Versova to the nearest train station at Andheri, about four kilometres away. The ting-ting of the bus conductor's bell as he signalled the driver to start or stop could be heard inside the house. An occasional bullock cart trundled down the dusty road in the late afternoon, and a few cars and lorries went by during the day.

Growing up, Rohini rarely saw her parents. Mostly she was in the company of her ayahs, siblings, and young cousins who visited the house now and again. Yet the sense of her parents' authority, especially Harshaba's, was ever present and Rohini had learned from an early age, through fear and devotion, to accept the strict regimen imposed by her mother.

Rohini's half-brother, Shrikant, had joined her father in business. Her brother, Mahesh, attended a boys' school at Andheri, but she and her two younger sisters, Sumitra and Amrita, were schooled at home by a procession of tutors who arrived each morning at first light. After lessons, and after the heat of the day had subsided, the girls were taken for games on the vast sandy beach below the house. On Saturdays they were sent on outings to the National Aquarium, the zoo, the Prince of Wales Museum, Vihar Lake, or the government dairy farm.

After Rohini's high school matriculation, Motilal and Harshaba were reluctant to allow her to attend college. What was the point in educating a girl who would eventually marry and live in her husband's household? Rohini's older sister, Saroj, was fourteen when given in marriage to a wealthy mill owner in Dantali; she had prospered without excessive education. At seventeen, Rohini was already getting past the marriageable age.

Rohini, although self-assured and strong-willed, knew better than to argue with her parents. But she was desperate for the opportunity to attend college and have a taste of the world that lay beyond her cocooned existence. She knew

Saroj had secretly wanted to attend college herself, and she enlisted her assistance: 'Education is the transmission of culture,' Rohini wrote. 'It is the soul of a society as it passes from one generation to another . . . My most beloved sister . . . please understand that I will be going to college for both of us.'

Motilal and Harshaba received a long letter from Saroj in which she explained that modern times demanded that girls attend college, and an education would make Rohini an ideal marriage prospect. Harshaba tossed her head and smirked – she'd learned everything about running a household from experience, not books, and the educated women she knew always put on airs – but Motilal asked Vincent to ready the car and drive him past all the colleges in Bombay. For more than an hour they toured the city's five or six leading colleges. Motilal liked the look of St Xavier's College; it was solidly built of good quality sandstone, and its heavy iron gates were not merely a decorative addition.

ಙ

On the first day of college an old servant called Balram was sent to drop Rohini. Despite the heat, Balram wore a fraying black suit coat over his loose-fitting work clothes. He would wait outside the college gate until classes let out and then escort Rohini home. They took the bus from Versova to Andheri, then the train to Marine Lines station, from where it was a short walk to the college. Past Princess Kulfi House, Shriram's Bangle Boutique, Kalachand's Saris, and Bombay Sporting Goods. Balram walking a few steps ahead kept glancing over his shoulder at his charge. Outside Metro Cinema, Rohini stopped to look at the film posters. When Balram tried to hurry her along, she said, 'I know my way from here. Don't you have a brother who works in the city? Why don't you go see him?' Balram protested loudly, he would never think of leaving her alone. She gave him some money, promised him more at the end of the week when she got her allowance if he would stop accompanying her every day. Balram finally agreed; he was poor and his wife in the village could use some new clothes.

Rohini made friends on the first day with two girls in her class – she sat with them in the canteen during morning break and they discussed lecture notes by the college gate for a few minutes before going home; but it did not occur to any of them that friendship could extend beyond the precincts of the college. Rohini's skin was lighter than theirs and her sari more costly, so they assumed she was of a higher birth.

Rohini had never been an outgoing person, preferring to read in her room or on a quiet bench in the garden, but the Cultural Group's poster at college about the music festival attracted her attention, and she went to the second floor auditorium to have a look. There was nothing grand about the auditorium – a modest wooden stage with blue velvet curtains and hundreds of metal folding chairs in neat, silent rows. But her heart leapt at the instruments on the stage – *tablas*, a harmonium and a *sitar*, solemn and graceful, holding the universe within them. She was overcome by a desire to share their mysteries. The next day she found the music supervisor, Mr Kelkar, in his office down a long corridor from the auditorium, and he assigned her to Hanif Hussein's group. 'Go quickly,' he said. 'The session has already begun.'

Slipping into the auditorium, she strode purposefully towards the stage and joined the group gathered on a dhurrie facing the harmonium. She liked the sound of singing voices, ebullient and confident, and she found it easy to pick up the familiar verses they sang, adjusting her voice to match the emotions she sensed they were striving for. As she sang with the class, she felt part of something greater, her presence in the world clear, yet inexplicable.

At home that evening, she draped a sequinned *dupatta* over her head and shoulders in the style of a seductive film actress, and, sitting before the full-length mirror, she practiced the raga, raising her right hand in classical style and swaying to the rhythm of her own voice.

Chapter 3

Hanif used his best fountain pen to write the message on a sheet of foolscap:

Dear Rohini,
Please stay for a few minutes after music practice to discuss details for the next festival.
    Sincerely,
    Hanif

The letters slanted backwards and also slightly forward, as though recoiling and springing ahead at the same time. He held the paper up, blew on it lightly, and then lining up the corners with care, folded the page several times until it was a thick four-inch square. As he wrote her name on the top his hand shook a little, so he added a small swirl to the 'R' where the ink had smudged.

He looked for Rohini in the college canteen during the mid-morning break. Students were streaming in for tea and samosas. The tea varied daily – too sweet or not sweet enough, too strong or too milky – but the *samosas* were always good and the smell of garlic and onions from the kitchen wafted like incense past the staff-rooms to the lecture halls on the far side of the building. The canteen was covered by corrugated-iron sheets and during the rainy season the drum of rain on metal made conversation impossible. But today the sun was shining and everyone was chattering. Every so often, the public address system hissed to life and announced forthcoming events. A small cement patio shaded by neem trees adjoined the canteen. There were a few benches and tables outside and even though Hanif didn't expect Rohini to be sitting there – the furniture was old, rusty, and splattered with bird droppings – he glanced outside anyway.

Rohini was standing by the tables, in line at the tea counter, in a yellow sari, her hair oiled and plaited with a white ribbon. Hanif fumbled with the folded note in his hand. He put it in his shirt pocket and took it out again. He glanced at her, saw her in profile and clutched the note with renewed determination. A gong announced the end of morning break as he approached her. Rohini turned to adjust her sari. A faint smile of recognition crossed her face. He thrust the note towards her. Puzzled, she accepted the folded paper, and stared at her name in ink smudged on the top. No one else noticed the exchange.

ನ

During the music session, Hanif was perspiring heavily and his voice sounded raspy. He offered no direction and let the class sing as they pleased. At the end, when everyone rose to leave, Hanif took longer than usual to stretch the cotton cover over the harmonium. The auditorium was emptying quickly and he could hear everyone talking and heading towards the door. He didn't dare look up. He half hoped she would leave with the others.

Rohini stood before him, fidgetting with the coloured glass bangles on her wrists. She pushed them up, but they slid down with a light clink as she straightened her arms.

Hanif swallowed, his mouth dry with fear, as he continued to adjust the cover, noticing that the edges of the cloth cover were dirty, and muttering, as if to himself, but also acknowledging her presence: 'Must take this home for a wash.'

'The festival,' Rohini said. 'You wanted to discuss something?' she said, coming a step closer. The stage floor creaked and, with that, the jingle of her anklets – chuum-chuum, chuum.

Hanif stared at her feet. He imagined her small ankles and the tiny silver bells that lay covered under the hem of her sari. 'Yes, the programme. We should plan . . .' Hanif's voice trailed off. 'I was thinking,' he said, more confidently now, his gaze moving upward to her face, 'we should sing a *jugalbandi*, a duet. The festival is still three weeks away. I was thinking of a song by Lata Dalat Mehmood. I will help you prepare.'

'Oh, no. I don't think . . .'

'Of course, it would mean a lot of practice.'

Hanif Hussein was known as the best musician in the college. A photo of him sitting before the harmonium was on the music festival's poster and only that morning she'd heard someone in the canteen say that Hanif was entered in a citywide music competition. And now he had picked *her*, a mere beginner, a first year student, to sing with him. He was obviously impressed with her voice. Further protest seemed wrong.

'Okay, it's settled then,' he said. 'You can stay behind for

an hour or so after the others leave. I'll let Mr Kelkar know.'
He offered to walk with Rohini to the station.

'Where do you live?' he said as they fell into step, he a
whole head taller than her.

'Near Andheri. At Versova.'

'Ah, Versova. That's quite far. I've never been there. What
subjects are you taking at college?'

'English,' she said.

'Have you thought about becoming a musician? You sing
well,' he said.

She didn't reply.

He glanced at her as she shifted the bag on her shoulder.
They approached a wet area on the pavement; she held the
pleats of her sari and stepped over the small puddles. They
passed Kayani's and his mouthed watered at the smell of
something baking that suffused the air. He made some
comment about mutton patties.

He liked his history class the best, he said. He wanted to
learn about 'real' people and 'real' events. He was skeptical of
literature, especially fiction. 'But poetry,' he said, 'poetry is
one of Allah's greatest gifts to mankind.'

They walked past the sari shops displaying yards of
fabric – green, yellow, red, purple – neatly pleated and
suspended from the awnings. Hanif had never paid attention
to the saris before. Now he made some banal statement
about the colours of the rainbow as he reached up and
trailed his fingers through the cloth.

He hoped to be a professional playback singer, he told
her, and she, for the first time looked at him directly.

'Really? Your voice will be in the pictures?' she asked.
'Actors will sing, and it will be your voice?'

'Yes,' he said, trying to sound casual.

'You'll be like Mukesh Kumar! You'll record songs in a studio?'

Inshallah, he thought, nodding happily. And then, as he glanced at her, he thought he caught a flicker of admiration in her eyes.

It was the hot season in Bombay. Hanif felt the sun on him, but he hardly minded. He looked sideways at Rohini and noticed her stepping intently, as though she were analyzing the irregularity of the stone footpath. He was afraid to look at her for too long, afraid that she might catch his eyes.

He didn't hear the cars and taxis blaring their horns, only the soft chuum-chuum of her anklets. He noticed the gentle hollows above her collarbone, and her skin, as soft and creamy as the flesh from a coconut. He felt guilty for the feelings she roused in him and kept chatting about inconsequential matters. He wondered whether she had any idea of the effect she was having on him.

They passed by a small roadside temple, its outside newly whitewashed, an intricate geometric pattern carved around its arched doorway. Instinctively, Rohini joined her hands and bowed her head. Hanif caught the fragrance of burning incense and camphor.

At Princess Kulfi House, Hanif wanted to suggest they go in for a kulfi. Pistachio was his favourite flavour. He stopped and looked at her and tried to think of the words and how to say them casually. His mouth grew dry. For a moment he thought she had materialized from the kulfi house and was made of cream and sugar. She might have sensed his hesitation, or anticipated the invitation and fretted. 'I must go now,' she said, and then hurried away, leaving him marooned between competing appetites.

At home in the music room that night Hanif sat on the floor before his harmonium and contemplated the instrument for a long time – the dark, polished case, the keyboard, the small piece of wood patterned with intertwined circles and curls that protected the inner workings and muted the higher frequencies. Reaching his fingers to the clasp at the back he undid the bellows that forced air over the reeds inside.

When his fingers took to the keys he was hardly aware of the notes he was playing. He tried to focus, tried to think of words to a ghazal, but instead, the music from the box at his feet brought thoughts of her. He replayed in his mind the walk from college to the station, recalling the deliberate lightness of their conversation. The way she said 'harmonium', how refined and mysterious the word sounded. His fingers slowed on the keys. Tomorrow he would tell the class about the romantic history of the harmonium – its invention in Paris a hundred years ago and how it was brought to India by the Christian missionaries as a tool for converting hearts to the religion of Jesus, and how they used it to seduce Muslims from Allah and the Prophet Mohammad and Hindus from Shiva and Ganesh – the class should know it was no ordinary instrument. Lifting his hand from the keyboard, he adjusted the knobs that let air into the chambers, and twirled the minor stops for a deeper pitch. He felt noble and important; he thrilled at recalling the look she'd given him when he said he was going to be a playback singer. His fingers took to the keys, and he closed his eyes, lifted his chin, and revelled in the glorious notes.

Chapter 4

Pervez found Hanif in the auditorium sitting before the harmonium, and was surprised to see Rohini sitting across him; this was a most unexpected scene. He quietly approached the stage, staying in the dark shadows.

'Tansen could create rain by singing the Megh Malhar raga,' Hanif said, 'and fire with the Dipak raga. Don't shake your head,' he said to Rohini. 'It's true. Tansen was a great musician, and the Moghul era was a great time of music.'

Pervez entered their sight line at the foot of the stage, his intrusion startling them both, and announced, like a harried messenger arriving breathless before the emperor in some grand costume epic film, 'President Roosevelt is dead.'

Hanif was annoyed at Pervez's interruption of their practice and began making minute adjustments to the harmonium to mask his irritation. 'So what if he's dead?' Hanif said. 'What do you want us to do? Go to his funeral?' He pumped the bellows and played several loud notes.

Pervez crossed the stage and slumped down into a chair, his hands hanging limp by his side. 'You know what Roosevelt said to the British PM?' Pervez asked.

Hanif ignored him. Rohini turned to Pervez with raised eyebrows.

Pervez sat forward, 'I heard him on BBC, Radio Ceylon. He said, "You can't fight a war against fascism and not work to free people all over the world from a backward colonial policy."'

Rohini said, 'In those exact words?'

'Yes, he wants to free everyone from colonialism – like President Lincoln and the slaves,' Pervez said.

Hanif kept playing, hoping that Pervez would leave. As a student of history, he knew major events were far more complicated than what simple phrases implied, and conflict over competing ideas came at a high price – an enormous cost in human lives, mostly those of largely innocent bystanders, and widespread destruction of property and culture.

Though Rohini seemed interested, Pervez grew angry at his friend's indifference to his news and he glared at Hanif before making a show of leaving the stage and stomping to the door. Another history paper was coming up and Pervez decided to write about Roosevelt and Churchill, and the Atlantic Charter at the Casablanca Conference.

'Now, where were we?' Hanif resumed, before the echoing slam of the door cut him off.

ৠ

Rohini was entranced by Hanif's deep, melodious voice, and the way he sang the ghazals with such conviction, such veneration. He would be famous one day, she felt sure of it, and the way he spoke to the music class was spellbinding.

'The word *alaap* means dialogue, or conversation. It is a conversation between the musician and the song.

The purpose of the alaap is to set the scene, create the moment.'

When the class began singing, he said over their voices, 'Don't be in a rush ... build up note by note.' And when they reached the end, he said, 'Sing it again. Remember, the alaap reflects the temperament of what is to come. It reveals the depth of a musician's training.' He was speaking to the whole class, but she thought he was speaking only to her.

She liked to watch him rotate his wrists and bend his hands this way and that before approaching the harmonium. She liked the way he closed his eyes and bowed in reverence to the instrument before he started playing. When his fingers scaled the keys, moving smoothly up and down, and, as the music drowned the air around them, she thrilled with anticipation of his first note.

His voice, her voice ... how grand it would be to sing with him at the festival. She would wear the orange sari with the gold border, and she would order a jasmine *gajra* for her hair. She decided not to invite anyone from home for the festival; there was no point. They would never approve of her singing in public.

Chapter 5

Dressing for the show, it had taken her three tries to get her sari on properly, the pleats too wide or too narrow as she tucked the fabric at her waist. She was afraid her voice would freeze, or she would forget the lines, or worst of all, get the lines mixed up with some other song and disgrace Hanif in front of the whole college. She had hardly eaten all day, a mistake she now realized; her stomach was churning and gurgling in the most awful way as she looked at the drawn curtain and how the spotlights beyond burned though a galaxy of tiny holes. The array of microphones around the instruments made her heart lurch. 'Does it change the voice?' she asked Hanif, who stood beside her backstage, humming, his head swaying gently from side to side. 'Should I sing softer?' Without looking at her, he shook his head and kept humming. The tension among the dozen or so other performers only heightened her own.

The giant curtain parted and she caught a glimpse of the crowded auditorium – hundreds of people dressed in their best evening clothes all cheering and applauding as Hanif and she walked on stage and into the blinding lights. The hoots and whistles from the back made her wish she had never agreed to sing in public. Hanif nodded to the sitar and tabla accompanists who were already at their positions on the far side of the stage. He seemed confident and composed, disconnected from the flourish of the moment. He smoothed his hands over his white *sherwani* and adjusted his vest before sitting down on the small carpet before the harmonium. She lowered herself onto the other carpet next to him, keeping her eyes down, nervousness clotting her throat.

Hanif played a scale on the harmonium. *Sa-Re-Ga-Ma-Pa-Dha-Ne-Sa* ... and back again ... *Sa-Ne-Dha-Pa-Ma-Ga-Re-Sa*. To Rohini the notes sounded both foreign and familiar. She adjusted the pleats of her sari around her knees. The house lights dimmed. In the audience, rustling and shuffling ceased. Hanif cleared his throat, leaned into the microphone and announced the title of the ghazal, first in Urdu, and then in English: '*Jeena hé Téré Muskurahat ké Leeyea* ... I Want to Live Only for Your Smile.'

The slow, quiet notes of the sitar, the tabla, and the harmonium started the song. Hanif's sonorous voice joined with the music and unfolded over the auditorium like yards of rich, luxurious brocade. Rohini's tender contralto voice came in on Hanif's cue, picking up the melody. His eyes were on the audience; his fingers moved on the keyboard with ease and grace. He caught a faint flowery scent from the gajra pinned in her hair. He could hear the light intakes of her breath, which the microphones would not detect.

Rohini wanted to look at him, to read some glimmer of approval on his face, but she didn't dare; her gaze stopped at the window nearest the stage, at the shadow cast by the big tamarind tree. Her voice didn't freeze, and she didn't forget the words, and she didn't get the lines mixed up with another song.

Something else happened.

She felt his voice passing over her, touching her skin like a vapour of cool mist, at first swirling unfettered around her, and then settling gently against her body. She felt his voice reaching into her, stimulating all her senses. The muscles in her neck grew taut with fear, joy, hesitation, delight. As their voices came together and the song picked up momentum, she gave her words to his. In the background, the beat of the tabla – *taka-dhan-taka-dhan-taka-dhan-dhan* – and with it, the reflective twang of the sitar. Together their voices refracted into myriad hues, his dipping into lower, darker, richer ranges, and hers soaring effortlessly to the higher, lighter, brighter registers of the musical palette.

She raised a nervous hand to adjust the gajra in her hair. *Taka-dhan-taka-dhan-taka-taka-dhan-dhan* – the tabla throbbed fast and loud.

He saw the white flowers, the petals wilting and turning brown at the edges. He saw her small wrist with the colourful bangles. He saw the semi-circular patch of perspiration under her arm and a sliver of her midriff below the sari blouse. Underneath the blouse he saw an outline – the soft roundness of her breast.

During the final refrain, she sensed his eyes searching her face, pursuing her thoughts. Around them – *taka-dhan-taka-dhan-taka-dhan-dhan* – the tablas kept on. She glanced at Hanif. He smiled. It was a smile full of colour, full of sparkling, tingling colour; it was the kind of smile to hide in her fist and bring out to savour when no one was looking.

Jeena hé téré muskurahat ké leeyea – she would live for his smile. After the last line of the song, after their voices reached a crescendo and the final note of the harmonium gave way to resounding applause, Rohini closed her eyes in breathless, bewildered surrender.

൭

At Chowpatty beach the next day, Hanif pointed to the farthest bench on the beach and said, 'Let's walk up to there. It's about a kilometre. Are you tired?'

Rohini shook her head. Six o'clock in the evening; she should have been on the train home by now. She would say she had to stay late for tutorials. They were in plain view of anyone driving down Marine Drive. She glanced at him, then quickened her steps and moved ahead. Did it look like they were walking *together*? She drew the end of her sari over her head, as though to shield herself from the sun.

'Wait,' he said, 'let me buy some *channas*.' He walked towards the *channa-walla* and she followed. She stood back as he spoke to him. Hanif handed her the cones and she held them, the newspaper warm in her palms, and watched as Hanif reached in his pocket for the coins. They walked in silence the rest of the way down the beach. Hanif pulled out an unironed handkerchief and brushed the sand off the bench before they sat.

'The sun will be setting soon,' she said. 'At Versova, the sunset is beautiful.'

'Oh, it must be a different sun over there,' he said, winking. 'Your house is by the beach?'

'Yes. It was built by a British architect.'

'Like the Buckingham Palace,' he said.

She laughed lightly.

'Do you have a changing of the guards?'

'We do have two chowkidars. The night chowkidar doesn't do much; he sleeps most of the time.' She laughed again as he threw a delighted glance at her.

'You looked good in your fancy sari yesterday,' he said. 'I think the programme was a success.'

'Was my voice alright? I was worried about the microphone.'

'Your voice was beautiful. You are beauti—' He stopped himself.

She knew what he was about to say. Her heart skipped and a fiery rush filled her head. The breeze lifted the end of her sari, and she let it slide off her head. Was he gazing at her? Curious about her own loveliness, she wanted to see herself sitting on the bench, see herself as he was seeing her. She looked straight ahead at the water, at the glowing sun that teetered teasingly at the very edge of the horizon. Gentle shades of red and orange stroked the sky. As the arc sank into the sea, the sky turned bright crimson and gold.

This must be a different sun, she thought. This was better than any other sunset she had seen.

Chapter 6

Hanif waited for Rohini outside the college canteen. He pretended to read the bulletin board, but there was only one notice on it, and everyone knew it had been there for days. He shifted from one foot to the other, walked to the end of the corridor and back as students streamed in and out of the canteen.

He motioned with his hand when he saw her, and then, as she walked hesitantly towards him, he posed the question that he'd rehearsed in his mind a thousand times: 'Would you like to see the new picture at Bandra Talkies? Tomorrow?' He said it softly and tried to conceal the eagerness in his voice but there was no mistaking it.

The shock on her face was only fleeting, but it sent his heart plummeting.

'Yes,' she whispered, then turned and quickly walked away.

ಐ

Shahjahan was the film playing. Rohini's eyes panned the theater, casting nervous glances at the faces in the audience. It was Sunday – at home she had said that two girls from college had invited her to the cinema. Harshaba suggested

she go by car since Vincent the driver was free, but Rohini
replied coolly that she had her train pass. Now as the lights
dimmed, she relaxed her shoulders and tried to settle into
the seat. On screen, the newsreel began with the headlines:
Rangoon victory celebrated while war goes on in Burma.
Over the sound of an army band, Lord Mountbatten,
Commander of Southeast Asia, inspected Indian, Nepalese
and British soldiers, and then stood at a podium saluting
smartly at the march-past. The troops had defeated the
Japanese and the jungle, the newscaster announced. Rohini
tried to pay attention, perhaps later she could discuss
something from the newsreel with Hanif, but there was
nothing other than the pomp and circumstance of the parade.
After two more short clips, the feature began and Hanif
exhaled in relief; she did the same. He glanced at her quickly
and shot her a smile. When Shahjahan appeared on screen
Rohini felt Hanif's arm brush against hers. The tension in
her shoulders returned and crept to her head, pressing on
her temples. She had no recollection of how the movie
started, but during Saigal's first song she felt Hanif's hand
on hers, his fingers curling lightly, naturally, over hers. Her
heart lurched and sent a sweet shock through her body. She
looked down at his hand resting on hers, and then her eyes
darted about the darkened hall. His grip grew more definite,
his thumb began stroking her hand; the images on screen
made little sense. At intermission, Hanif asked if she wanted
to go to the lobby for snacks; she insisted they remain in
their seats. If she were found out . . . she didn't dare think of
the consequences.

೧೧

Pervez looked at Hanif and Rohini sitting across from him at Café Royal. He knew they had gone to the cinema together. He recalled Hanif's excitement and that he had told his friend, 'Cancel the plan. Hanif, *you've* obviously lost your mind, but Rohini too . . .?'

Café Royal was a small Irani restaurant with old marble-top tables and rickety chairs. The porcelain cups and saucers were chipped, the spoons smudged. Most people came for tea and sweets. Some afternoons one could get a single or double omelette with a side plate of bread and butter. Hanif ordered tea for the three of them, and *jalebis* in honour of Pervez's birthday.

Pervez wondered how long his friends could continue their dalliance before being found out, and he secretly hoped it would be soon. The day after their debut, Pervez was being asked, 'Is anything going on with those two?' He had shrugged, annoyed that he was the one left to make excuses for them.

The owner of Café Royal, who was also the cook, was in the kitchen. His helper, a thin boy of ten or eleven, sat on a wooden stool in front of a grimy glass case containing a mound of brightly coloured sweets. A metal tray lined with newspapers held freshly fried samosas, the oil still glistening on the triangular peaks. The boy waved his arms half-heartedly to keep the flies away.

Outside, the rain had abated and the wet smell of the pavement now mixed with the odour of burnt sugar and spices from inside the shop. The sound of Hindi film music came from one of the neighbouring shops.

'Look,' Pervez said unfolding a newspaper and holding it

up so they could see the headline: *Muhammad Ali Jinnah seeks Muslim nation state.* 'Listen, these are Jinnah's words.' He moved his teacup aside and read aloud:

> Never have we in the whole history of the League done anything except by constitutional methods. But now we bid goodbye to constitutional methods. We have exhausted all reason. There is no tribunal to which we can go. The only tribunal is the Muslim nation.

He looked up from the paper at them questioningly. Rohini pushed the plate of jalebis towards Pervez. 'Come on, eat. They're still warm.'

'Let me see,' Hanif said, reaching for the newspaper. He glanced at the photo of Jinnah – suit and tie, an earnest, respectable face. Hanif scanned the opening paragraphs. 'He's a brilliant man.'

Pervez raised his eyebrows and asked, 'You're in favour of Partition?'

Hanif said to Pervez, 'Look what happened in Calcutta last week. Riots, thousands killed. Religion and politics have become intertwined.' Hanif considered the jalebis for an instant, and nudged the plate to the middle. 'Partition may be the only way to pacify the people.' He folded the newspaper carefully and returned it to Pervez. 'The riots in Calcutta were only the beginning. The violence will spread around the country.'

Rohini looked at Hanif in disbelief. That Hanif was Muslim troubled her, mostly because she knew her parents would not approve. Not to mention the way her oldest brother, Shrikant, spoke about Muslims. 'India's nightmare,' she had overheard him say just recently. 'They think of themselves as Muslims first, and then as Indians. They are the root of the problem. If they've acquired a minority complex, it's their own fault.' But whenever she read Hanif's letters, or the tempered notes of the harmonium filled her thoughts, she managed to put aside her worries. Now, as Hanif mentioned 'riots' and 'violence', the fact that he was Muslim seemed suddenly magnified.

'The Muslim League will push us to civil war,' Pervez said.

Hanif shifted in his chair, then stated with emphasis what he'd heard his father say a dozen times: 'Jinnah has been a true Indian nationalist, but he has always been the one to compromise for the sake of Hindu-Muslim unity.' He took a sip of tea. 'A separate Muslim nation is a reasonable way out. Partition is the only realistic solution.'

'Partition?' Pervez leaned away from the table, his voice rising in anger. 'That is not the answer!'

'Please,' Rohini raised her hands to silence them. 'No politics today. Okay?' She asked Pervez, 'Is your mother cooking something special for you tonight?'

'Yes. Prawn curry,' Pervez said, without enthusiasm.

'Do you like fish, Hanif?' she asked.

'Yes. But mutton *biryani* is my favourite,' he replied.

Rohini had never eaten fish or meat; everyone in her family was vegetarian.

They lapsed into silence. Outside, it was raining again. Rohini stared at the cups on the table. A thin, milky skin had formed on her tea. She skimmed it off with her teaspoon, raised the cup to her mouth and took a sip, barely aware of the sweetness. Pervez said that it was getting late, but no one moved. The jalebis lay untouched on the table, the yellow syrup forming small sticky dots on the plate.

ಬಿ

Hanif and Pervez took a bus to the Versova fishing village the following Sunday. Pervez wanted Hanif to see Rohini's house from the outside. It might prompt him to give up his hopes for her.

Just after the 'Seven Bungalows' bus stop, when the house came into view, Pervez asked the bus driver to go slow past the big house. He nudged Hanif, who sat up straight and trained his eyes to where Pervez was pointing. The driver told them in a deferential tone, 'That – there – is Sagar Mahal. Where Chimanji-sahib lives. It took three years to build the house. It is painted yellow every year.'

The house was far bigger than Hanif had anticipated, and he was struck by its quiet grandeur. Wide verandahs surrounded the front of the house. A tall fountain stood in the garden and palm trees bearing clusters of coconuts loomed gracefully upwards along the driveway. There were garages to one side, a pillared porch, and steps lined with flowerpots leading to the house. A covered walkway ran to what looked like a guesthouse, twice the size of Hanif's own home.

At the fishing village, while they waited for another bus to take them back, Hanif said to Pervez, 'In a few months, after I graduate, Inshallah . . . oh, I don't know, sometime in the future, I will marry her. I see myself in wedding regalia, in a silk sherwani and embroidered shoes arriving at the gates of Sagar Mahal. The outside of the house will be decorated with streams of flowers and coloured lights; there'll be lanterns hanging in the trees and rose petals perfuming the fountain. Music from sitars, tablas, and *tanpuras* will fill the air, and there'll be hundreds of guests, from her side and mine . . .'

Pervez stared at Hanif. What was happening to the world? 'Hanif, you're an idiot. You've gone *ab-so-lute-ly* mad,' he said. 'She's Hindu. Don't you see? This is India!' Pervez drew his right index finger across his throat.

But Hanif persisted in being rhapsodic, impervious to reason. As a recording artist he would earn plenty of money. He had connections at All India Radio and HMV Gramophone. He would introduce Rohini to his parents after graduation. There was the Hindu-Muslim issue, yes, but they would overcome that somehow. As for *her* parents . . . she never talked about them, but once they realized his potential for greatness, they would *most* definitely be pleased.

Pervez tried again. 'A nice Muslim wife – your parents will find one for you.' When Hanif shook his head, Pervez said, 'There's a building on Lamington Road. I've heard it's a clean, discreet place where the girls are . . .'

Hanif glared at Pervez, then turned his head and spat on the ground. 'Good-for-nothing bloody fool!'

Chapter 7

On the day of Hanif's graduation, atom bombs were dropped on Japan, first on Hiroshima and then Nagasaki, and the cities and the people who lived in them were obliterated in an instant. There was no college assembly; all the students were out in the streets, raising money for a Japanese relief fund. Hanif and Rohini stood with a small group near the intersection at Dhobi Talao, holding red cans with two-inch slots in the lids, the warring odours of vehicle fumes and roasting corn engulfing them. It was the rainy season in Bombay, and ordinarily they would have complained about the drenching downpours and the muddy roads, but they looked up at the wet sky with indifference. What had been done to the Japanese, no matter that they were at war, was beyond belief. As the shock at the use of such awesome power abated, there was urgency in the way everyone talked about history and politics and tried to make sense of the new world; it suddenly seemed that nothing mattered anymore, for everything that was important could perish in a second, leaving in its aftermath little but profound sorrow.

Hanif began working at All India Radio, where he catalogued music according to genre and artist, and on Fridays wrote a music review for the station manager to broadcast on Saturday afternoons. It was a quiet, easy job that gave him a modest income and allowed enough time at the end of the day to practice his own music. He would marry Rohini. He had no notion of proposing to her; between them marriage was a tacit agreement but the customary details involving their families seemed too formidable to worry about just now.

At home he spent his time at the harmonium practicing for the music competition. Winning the recording contract was uppermost in his mind. He had a new music teacher, Iqbal Mehmood, a polite, middle-aged man, whom his father had met through a colleague at the accounting firm where he worked.

Hanif looked forward to the times every now and then when he would meet Rohini for tea or to see a movie. He wrote her letters, which he sent through Pervez. Penned on lined, full or half sheets of paper, the letters concluded with a few lines of poetry from Faiz or Tagore, and sometimes the verses were followed by his own initials, 'H.H.'

Rohini kept all his letters, wrapping them in a silk *rumal*, carefully knotting the diagonal corners of the cloth, and then hiding the bundle behind the folded saris and petticoats in her armoire. On Sundays, when there was no college, she selected one or two letters from the silken bundle, placed them within the pages of Defoe, or Keats, or Shelley, and re-read them furtively.

৩৩

Rohini waited for Hanif at the news kiosk on the railway platform. Newspapers were stacked in stringed bundles and she glanced at the headlines. She checked her watch. There was no sign of him and she walked to the main entrance from where she could see the bus stop on the opposite side. Three buses later there was still no sign of Hanif.

She left the station and, with nothing to do, she wandered aimlessly, passing Rajabai Tower, noticing its coffered walls, stained glass windows, and heavy cornices. She walked past an empty bicycle stand, a graffiti-covered alley, and a bookshop, its shutter half closed. As she turned back for the station, she heard the familiar voice, 'Rohini, wait.' Through the ambling crowd she glimpsed Hanif running up the footpath, dodging and darting between people, his arm raised and waving. She smiled and tried to smooth her hair.

'The Navy has gone on strike,' Hanif said, trying to catch his breath. 'They're protesting against the British. Poor service conditions and discrimination.' He panted as he spoke. 'Many navy officers have been arrested. All the roads around the harbour area are barricaded. Everyone has taken to the streets.' His white shirt was soaked with sweat; a blotch of blue ink from a leaky fountain pen marked his shirt pocket. 'I couldn't get a bus; the trams have also stopped. I came as fast as I could.' Hanif wiped the sweat on his forehead with his palm. 'A naval mutiny! Imagine!'

Rohini could feel his warm breath – it smelled of fennel seeds and betel nut – and she was content to stand there and revel in the halting sequence of his words.

'Come on,' he said, taking her hand and pulling her towards the station. 'We must go before they stop the trains.' As they raced through the side gate into the station, they heard the voice over the public address system announcing the times of the last departing trains before the lines would be stopped. Even the boot-polish boys were packing up their boxes, and the cold drink vendor was moving his crates inside the booth, the bottles clanging against each other. 'Hurry,' Hanif said turning to Rohini, and as they approached the bridge over the platform they took the steps two at a time.

There was barely enough standing room in the train. Rohini held on to a side railing, and scanned the other faces, worried as always that someone might see her with Hanif. The train swayed as it picked up speed, the wind whipping through the compartment, the wheels furiously grinding the tracks. Marine Lines. Grant Road. Charney Road. She could feel the dampness of Hanif's shirt and smell the perspiration of his body. Her eyes focused on the ink stain on his shirt pocket – a miniature map of Africa – she wanted to trace her fingers over the blue mark.

Hanif said, 'I wonder what the Congress leaders will say about the strike?'

'Everyone knows what Gandhi will say,' Rohini replied. 'He'll condemn the riots and the mutiny. Nehru will support the strike. And Sardar . . . who ever knows?'

'Remember last week when the British arrested that Indian officer? He got a seven-year sentence for doing nothing,' Hanif said, shaking his head. 'I think it's going to happen.' A southbound train thundered by.

'What's going to happen?' she said.

'The British will have to hand everything over to India,' he said, raising his voice over the clamour of the tracks.

'I know,' she said. It was all everyone was talking about at college. 'News of the strike will be on the BBC this evening,' she said.

'Tomorrow, most likely,' he said with authority, 'by the time they hear about it in London.'

The train slowed. Rohini looked about the compartment nervously.

They stood quietly for a while, the turmoil of the city behind them. Khar, then Santacruz, then Vile Parle – the stations went by much too fast. At Andheri they got off the train and stood outside Bata Shoes for a few minutes. Hanif wanted to ride the bus with her to Versova. 'No,' she said.

He wanted to tell her that he'd seen her house from the outside, but he felt awkward suddenly. '*Khuda hafiz,*' he said instead, and immediately wondered why he'd said the Muslim farewell to her. She looked at him in question. 'It means goodbye,' he said. 'Actually it means, "May God keep you safe."'

She repeated the phrase to herself as she walked away. She turned and called out to him, 'Khuda hafiz, Hanif.'

II

DIAMONDS

Chapter 8

Harshaba stood in the divankhana, feet apart and hands on hips, a commander in the field, ordering the servants to beat the sofa cushions properly, to polish the carved wood tables with extra care. She marched to the kitchen and gave instructions for the food, and personally washed the never-used tea service from Japan, arranging the leaf-patterned cups on a large tray so the cup handles pointed the same way. Marching back to the divankhana, she switched on the chandeliers and stepped this way and that, craning her neck to check each of the light bulbs for any sign of dust or flicker. Important guests were coming for tea.

Motilal ignored his wife's bluster and posturing and decided to enjoy the afternoon. He was immensely proud. The silk business had expanded to Bangalore, he had built a palace of a house on the beach, and now he had negotiated an excellent marriage for his second daughter into a prominent family. He maintained two houses he owned in Ahmedabad – ancestral residences – a spacious villa on rolling acres on the banks of the Sabarmati, and another in the labyrinthine heart of the old city in Khajoori-ni-Pol. To him, they were not property but a responsibility; the family roots in Gujarat could not be sundered. 'Someday, the British might force us to leave Bombay,' he said frequently to Harshaba. With the end of the war and the growing calls from Indians of all political colours for Independence, 1946 had been an uncertain year and the future was too murky to take risks. But now, as he walked about the divankhana surveying the preparations, he suddenly felt lighthearted and eager for the guests to arrive.

Harshaba swept into Rohini's room carrying a bright sari, the colour of turmeric, and heavy gold jewellery. 'My dear,' she said, putting an arm around Rohini, 'you must look beautiful. Here, I've brought you my favourite necklace.' Harshaba rarely showed affection and for a moment Rohini was surprised at her motherly gesture and the genuine tone of her voice. 'Come, let me help you,' Harshaba said, stroked her daughter's hair, and abruptly left to tend to other preparations.

Rohini knew that the guests were coming with a marriage proposal. She would have to play along. As she opened the folded sari and watched the fabric billow to the floor, she felt detached and ashamed of her luxurious existence. Independence and Partition were imminent. She stared wanly at the sari; mutinies and riots raged in the streets and she was expected to look serene. She stared at the face powder and *kajal* in the dressing table drawer. After running the comb through her hair a few times, she braided it and put on her mother's necklace but didn't bother glancing in the mirror. She switched on the radio and smiled at the song, singing along to Saigal as she wandered aimlessly around the room, her shoulders swaying a little to the music. Finally she sank into the armchair by the window. The sea was a shining steel-grey expanse. When would she see Hanif again? It had been three days since their last meeting. The greatest consolation was that Hanif's family had no intentions of immigrating to Pakistan. That fact alone buoyed her spirits from time to time. She imagined herself with Hanif, strolling on Chowpatty Beach and in the gardens at Malabar Hill, taking a picnic to Powai Lake, and watching movies at Metro and Bombay Talkies – everything in openness, with no worry of reprisal. She imagined days when they would practice music for hours at a stretch. He'd described the music room at his house and she imagined them there, rehearsing for another concert, far grander than the college festival. They would be a team, the two of them creating a new musical ethos in the city.

At a few minutes past four o'clock that November afternoon, Sonabhai and Suluben Shah of Ahmedabad arrived at Sagar Mahal. The Shahs were diamond merchants with shops in Bombay, Ahmedabad, and Delhi. Their twenty-three-year-old son, Jagmohan, would soon be returning from South Africa, where he had spent two years learning the diamond business in Johannesburg. He was their only son and would inherit a business empire.

Motilal and Harshaba led their two guests into the divankhana that stretched all the way to the back of the house. Sonabhai stopped at the doorway and surveyed the space slowly. He took in the good furniture, the sepia photos, the marble floors, and then angled his neck to the high ceiling and the chandeliers, which were sparkling with light. The large windows were thrown open for the afternoon party, and the sea air blew in slow, steady gusts.

Sonabhai breathed deeply. He was a thin man in a white dhoti and beige jacket; the turban tied loosely on his head, made him appear tall and full. 'It's a palace,' he said, turning to his wife. Suluben, an elegant woman in a beige sari, nodded and walked towards the bluish porcelain statue of a Chinese man that stood solemnly on a low table.

'He's from the time of our forefathers, something they acquired in their travels,' Motilal explained, running his fingers over the long beard and flowing blue robe.

'An antique,' Suluben said, leaning forward to take a closer look. 'Such exquisite colouring of the clothing.'

They settled into the sofas, the men on one side, the women in the settee across from them. Motilal asked how Sonabhai managed his shops in three different cities, how business had fared during the war. Sonabhai's answer was animated, waving his arms as he talked, his turban unravelling a little as he nodded. Leaning towards Motilal, he asked why they had such an unusual surname – did it have anything to do with China? Motilal explained that the Chimanjis were pioneers in bringing silk to India from China along the silk route. He and his brother had lived in Shanghai for several years to get the business established. 'Ah, Shanghai,' Sonabhai said, but Motilal changed the topic and soon had Sonabhai boasting about his son. 'In South Africa, Jagmohan worked at a huge diamond company of which we hold a thirty per cent share. Our partners are Europeans, from Amsterdam, and they couldn't pronounce his name, so they called him "Jag", which he rather liked and has used ever since.' Sonabhai let out a brief chuckle, as if inviting them to share in his son's whimsical side. 'My son knows everything about the diamond business,' he said, to dispel any misapprehension that Jag was not earnest and hardworking. Motilal nodded in approval.

In the presence of their husbands, both women had their saris drawn over their heads. Harshaba glanced at Suluben's hands, expecting them to be covered in diamonds. But there was only a thin gold band on one finger and two simple bangles on her wrists. If Harshaba was disappointed, she didn't let on. She edged herself closer to her guest on the small settee. 'Rohini goes to *college*. We believe in educating our daughters, you see; we're modern people. And she's good in music. She sings – not film songs, but classical music, and never in public.' Suluben smiled widely.

The snack dishes were cleared away and a servant brought in the tea tray and set it on the centre table before an empty chair. The side door into the divankhana opened slowly.

Rohini, eyes to the floor and one hand holding the end of the sari over her head, stepped into the silence. She should be nervous, she thought, but as she approached the guests, she felt weighed down by the realization that she was deceiving these people who had come to see her. She bowed and touched the feet of the two visitors, and went to the tea tray. Her movements were steady and graceful as she picked up the teapot. She knew the visitors were watching her. The steam rising from the cups smelled pleasingly of mint. She poured a dash of milk, stirred in the sugar. Then a thought popped unbidden into her head: What if these were Hanif's parents? Her hands shook, the cup rattled and tea sloshed into the saucer the moment she offered it to Suluben.

'It's a beautiful sari,' Suluben said to cover the mishap.

'It's from Banaras,' Harshaba said, a little too loudly,

before turning her attention to the door where Shrikant and his wife Prema, Mahesh, and Sumitra and Amrita were waiting.

'I thought there are four sisters,' Suluben said.

'Yes,' Harshaba said. 'My oldest daughter, Saroj, couldn't come today. She lives in Dantali. I'm sure you'll meet her next time.'

Suluben handed Harshaba a small bundle wrapped in red cloth, which she said was her son's horoscope. Harshaba smiled, her hands clasping Suluben's as she accepted the bundle. Rohini, observing the exchange, was reminded of the bundles containing Hanif's letters. He'd signed the early missives *yours sincerely*; then, *your friend*; and after they held hands at the theater, *your beloved*. She glanced at her parents, at the smiling guests. It felt to her like a scene from a film – she was not, however, the heroine, but standing at a distance, outside the frame.

৵৵

Harshaba summoned the pujari the following day. He sat cross-legged on the floor on a white sheet studying the two small booklets for a long time. Absently he stroked his greying beard as he read each booklet separately, then set them side by side and compared each page. When he finally looked up, he found Harshaba staring at him, a stern look on her face. He cleared his throat. Jagmohan's and Rohini's constellations were in different *rajjus*, which was a good thing, he said. There wasn't a noticeable difference in their lifespans, their mental temperaments were complimentary, good physical health for both, and, there was promise of at least one progeny, more if they performed a series of *pujas* to Shiva. Harshaba sighed loudly. The pujari closed the horoscopes, collected his money and left.

Harshaba spent the afternoon sequestered in the upstairs storeroom, taking inventory of the jewels and finery. Rohini's trousseau was almost ready – brocades from Banaras, *kanjivarams* from Madras, and *patolas* from Pathan; bangles, necklaces, and hairpieces studded with emeralds, rubies, diamonds, pearls. Obsessively, Harshaba arranged and rearranged, counted and re-counted everything. More than once she went out onto the verandah and squinted down the road looking for Motilal's car.

Enclosed in a small envelope with Jagmohan's horoscope, Harshaba had been surprised to find his photograph. She held the photo carefully. He was a fine-looking man with fair skin and a straight nose. But his spectacles worried Harshaba. 'Looking closely at all those diamonds must have ruined his eyes,' she said to Motilal.

'He comes from a good family and the horoscopes match,' Motilal said. 'What more do you want?'

ಬಌ

Prema, Rohini's sister-in-law, found her sitting quietly at her desk. 'A wedding in the family,' she gushed, putting her arms around Rohini. She was thin and tall, her posture sentry-like. Shrikant and Prema were married a few years ago, and every day Harshaba asked Prema whether she was pregnant and perhaps it was time to perform a puja if she wasn't.

Rohini smiled weakly at Prema. Although Rohini rarely spoke to Shrikant, who was more than ten years older than her, she was fond of his wife. Prema was good-natured and jovial, at least whenever Harshaba wasn't around. 'I'm afraid of her,' Prema confided to Rohini during the early days of her marriage, and Rohini had tried in vain to reassure her. Should she tell Prema about Hanif? Should she tell Prema how he arched his eyebrows and lifted his head when he sang, and the way he took her hand, gently yet matter-of-factly, as though she *belonged* to him? 'The thing is . . .' Rohini began, but her voice faltered.

'They probably have a big house in Ahmedabad,' Prema said. 'Ahmedabad is a nice place, but you will miss Bombay.'

'Yes,' Rohini said, looking distractedly at the coconut palms outside the window. She had always liked the palms, the way they loomed and curved upward, their fronds swaying and swishing with the breeze. But today they were simply tall and crooked.

'At least you'll be close to Dantali. You can visit Saroj,' Prema said.

'Yes.'

'Come,' Prema said. 'It's time for dinner.'

Rohini followed Prema to the dining room. She sat with Prema and her sisters and listened to their easy chatter. Prema tapped the edge of Rohini's *thali*. 'Don't worry,' she said. 'Once you see your husband, your appetite will return.'

That night Rohini lay restless under the mosquito net. The night was cool, but she pushed away the quilt and it lay bunched in a heap at her feet. Hanif. How would she tell her parents about him? How would she face her mother's wrath, and her father's disappointment? She had known for many years that they would find a suitable man for her. How easily Saroj, her elder sister, had taken on the role of a married woman. And Saroj had been only fourteen then. Nothing made sense. When sleep finally overtook her tired mind, the temple bells across the road were chiming and the first bus from Andheri had rumbled past the house to the fishing village.

That evening, on returning from college, she reached in the armoire for Hanif's letters and, hiding them under her arm, making sure her sari covered her shoulder properly, she fled to the back garden and found the farthest bench. She read and reread the letters until the sun slipped away and fierce shades of red and amber swept the sky.

ಬಬ

'Cook everything in ghee today,' Harshaba said to the cook who had just returned from the market laden with cabbages, brinjals, spinach, and cauliflowers. 'Use the good rice from the cupboard. Add extra saffron in the *halva*.' The Shahs were coming to Sagar Mahal again, this time with Jagmohan and his two sisters. And this time, for dinner.

On Sundays, it was always *dal-dhokli* for lunch and *khichdi* for dinner, and although Rohini didn't particularly care for either, she liked the simplicity of these Sunday meals. Today, the visitors had upset the routine. She resented the thick smell of frying onions and chilli from the kitchen.

The servants scurried about, fetching or cleaning this and that. Harshaba brought out the whole silver dining set, and, after wiping everything with a damp cloth, carefully counted the varying sizes of spoons. She instructed the chowkidar to festoon the front gate with orange and yellow marigolds. But when Motilal saw the elaborate display, he asked the chowkidar to take everything down. 'No need for such a show,' he said to Harshaba.

That evening everyone gathered in the divankhana. As arranged, Motilal, Harshaba, Sonabhai and Suluben, Shrikant and Prema, settled into the sofas in the centre of the divankhana. Rohini, Mahesh, Sumitra and Amrita, along with Jagmohan and his two sisters went to the less-formal anteroom adjoining the main hall.

Rohini avoided Jagmohan's glances. She turned away and tried to compose her breathing, which seemed to be coming in short heavy gasps. She felt Jagmohan's eyes appraising her. A muscle in her neck twitched. She kept her gaze focused on the floor and tried to imagine herself not in the room at all.

Jagmohan had brought a gift for Rohini, a rectangular box wrapped in glossy white paper with red string, but instead of giving it to her directly, he placed it casually on the marble side table, beside the porcelain vase.

She glanced at him quickly as he sat in an armchair across from her. A grey-blue, English-style suit. Her breathing came in uneven gasps again. He finished his glass of rose water and set it back on the tray. His sisters were both small and thin with round, smiling faces. Everyone around her was talking. One of the sisters was going to play in a badminton tournament, and the other was going abroad, to London, to visit an aunt. Jagmohan fidgeted, twisting back and forth the strap of his rectangular watch on his wrist.

Rohini heard Mahesh and Jagmohan talking about cricket, the merits of the Indian team captain and the recent matches against England. She heard Jagmohan laughing. It was a quiet, confident laugh. 'By the way,' he said, 'please call me Jag.' Jag – what a name. It sounded contrived and silly, even though she guessed it was meant to be stylish and modern. She glanced at him again. A wide forehead, neatly trimmed moustache, and thin, black-rimmed glasses; his dark, oiled hair was parted at the side, and brushed straight back.

'What exactly was your work in Johannesburg?' Mahesh asked.

'I studied diamonds . . . I attended meetings with the other partners . . .' Jag waved a dismissive hand in the air, shifted in the chair, and crossed one leg over the other, all of which Rohini took to mean he was not one to discuss business in front of women.

Her eyes settled on his polished shoes and the design of tiny holes looping over the black leather. Under her feet, which were bare, the floor felt smooth and familiar.

'The process, though, is rather interesting,' Jag said. 'Hundreds of tonnes of granite and kimberlite are dug up from the ground and sent through a series of crushers to extract the diamonds. They're anywhere from one millimetre to thirty in size, which means anywhere from a grain of sand to a ping-pong ball. We organize them in categories, and decide which ones to send for cutting and polishing, which ones are suitable for industrial use, which ones for jewellery. They look like insignificant pebbles when they're first excavated, nothing like what you see in the shops.'

Casting careful sideways glances, Rohini watched Jag as

he spoke. She wanted to think him tedious and boring, but she knew that he was poised and charming and dignified – straight out of a Jane Austen novel set in India. She heard her mother's reproachful voice in her head criticizing the useless college books on her desk. Yet Harshaba had picked a man for her who was a character from those very books.

'South Africa is a beautiful country,' Jag said. 'But the government is another story. There's a horrible tension between the blacks and the whites and the Indians.'

'Really?' Mahesh said. 'Worse than the Muslim problem here?'

'Muslim problem? I don't know,' Jag said. 'Well, I don't know any Muslims personally, and I don't think my parents do either. There are large communities of Muslims in Ahmedabad – one cannot help but hear their towers blasting four times a day – but, you know how it is, we have no reason to mix with them.'

Rohini's throat tightened.

'I knew some Muslim boys in school,' Mahesh said. 'Poor, but decent chaps.'

'I say, it is rather warm today,' Jag said. 'May I remove my coat?' His question was addressed to Rohini, who nodded her assent and watched through down-turned eyes as he stood up to remove his suit jacket, which he hung over the back of his chair, then sat down again, being careful not to lean back. Damp circles had formed on his white shirt under his armpits. He reached up and touched the knot of his broad-striped tie. She noticed his neat, rounded fingernails and his long, knobby hands. For a moment she felt sorry for him; sorry he had journeyed from Ahmedabad to Bombay; sorry for the trouble he had taken to dress in a suit.

'What about the customers at your shops? Surely there are Muslims among them,' Mahesh said.

'Muslims go to their own jewellers,' Jag said. 'They will never buy diamonds from us. They think we are out to cheat them, and don't know the meaning of a fair price.'

Rohini resented how flippantly he judged Muslims. She wanted to say something in defense but nothing came to mind. Besides, he had spoken with authority, and although she knew about Christianity from the novels she'd read, she hardly knew anything about Islam. She knew of the Prophet and that his teachings were based on divine revelations; that Muslims went on pilgrimage in Arabia, from Mecca to Medina; their festivals were Id and Ramadan, but she had no idea what the festivals commemorated. She had never seen a Koran, and she had never been inside a mosque. She knew, however, that when she married Hanif, she would have to convert . . .

Suddenly, Jag's sisters were standing, and Sumitra and Amrita and Mahesh were too – they were going to the back garden to look at the sea. 'You both stay here and talk,' Mahesh said. Rohini thought her heart had stopped. Now she would have to sit here alone with him.

'Rohini,' Jag said.

She sat upright in her chair with her eyes to the floor.

There was a long silence before he said, 'What have you read in college? Daniel Defoe?'

'Yes. *Robinson Crusoe*,' she said, surprised that he knew of Defoe. She looked up at him quickly.

'What else?' Jag asked.

She felt bouts of dizziness come and go. 'We've read a novel by Shelley . . . *Frankenstein*,' she managed.

'And?'

'And Jane Austen. Also, French authors in English translation. Hugo, Balzac, Flaubert.' Rohini had written in her notes that morning: 'Flaubert's tragic heroine is a hopeless, pitiful romantic with no grasp on reality; but throughout the narrative she remains completely fascinating.' Right now, when she tried to think of Flaubert's novel and the name of his heroine, nothing came to mind.

'What about poetry? Wordsworth, Keats?'

'Yes, of course,' she replied, surprised again that he knew these names. Did he read them? She felt a flicker of respect for him.

'You enjoy poetry?' Jag asked.

'Yes,' she said. 'We have a good teacher. Father Almeida. He studied at Oxford.' She thought of Father Almeida, in the white habit of a Franciscan, lecturing on the Romantics. She recalled his passionate description of the English countryside – thatch-roofed cottages, cobbled roads, green pastures, and a docile drizzle covering everything. When she tried to imagine the English landscape, what came to mind instead were the rolling hills of the small resort in the Deccan where she had been two or three times on family holidays.

'I think our Indian poets are remarkable,' Jag said.

'Ah, yes. Tagore,' she said.

'And Faiz, Iqbal, Ghalib . . . there are so many.'

'You read Urdu?' Rohini could not hide the disbelief in her tone. She looked at him for a long moment.

'A little. I would like to study it more systematically. I also want to learn music. Piano or violin. I went to a symphony concert in Johannesburg. And you? You're interested in music, they told me,' he gestured to the divankhana where their parents were sitting, and from where the sounds of conversation and laughter drifted towards them.

'Yes,' she said. Music was the last thing she wanted to talk about with Jag. Leaning forward in the chair, she said, 'You were saying about the government in South Africa . . .'

'Oh yes, South Africa. The people – whites, blacks, Indians – all segregated,' Jag said, making three compartments in the air with his hands. 'Sometimes the blacks are treated worse than animals,' he grimaced. 'Many of them have formed underground resistance movements. They have no money but they are quite well organized. I knew this man . . .'

She cut him off. 'But what does that have to do with Hindus and Muslims here?' Rohini could hardly believe she had let herself be drawn into a conversation with this man. What did she care about his opinion of Hindus and Muslims? She wanted to tell him right away that she had no intentions of marrying him. He would be offended, but what did it matter? She looked at him straight in his face for the first time.

Jag cleared his throat. 'The violence. Well, actually, I don't know. It's all very complicated, isn't it? Hindus, Muslims, the British in India . . . you're interested in politics,' he said, and Rohini was certain she detected a hint of suspicion, if not awe, in his voice. He folded his arms over his chest. 'To tell you the truth,' he paused, and sat straighter, 'I've been reading a great deal lately, about Indian history. Since the time of the Moghul period,' he paused again, looked gently at Rohini, 'it has been inevitable that India would be divided. Hundreds of years ago, before they converted, the Muslims here used to be Hindus. And with the Portuguese and British missionaries, thousands became Christians, both Catholic and Protestant. What I'm coming to believe is that religion . . .'

Jag droned on, his words and his presence a constant reminder of her unfortunate predicament. Rohini stared at her lap – at the pair of gold lion-mouthed bangles on her wrists – as the first lines of the song she had sung with Hanif for the college festival came into her head. She was on stage, under the lights, the harmonium between them, their voices in unison. Empowered by the thought, she resolved to end this alliance with Jag, or Jagmohan, or whatever his name was. She hoped he and his parents would leave right after dinner so she could retreat to her room and her books.

Chapter 9

In Ahmedabad, on the evening of Makar Sankranti, the entire city was on the terraces and rooftops and looking skyward as strong winds sent hundreds of kites soaring. Green, yellow, pink, orange, purple – the colours patterned the sky. The festival marked the new moon when the sun passed through the winter solstice, from the Tropic of Cancer to the Tropic of Capricorn.

'That is special *manja*,' Jag said to Rohini, pointing to a big spool of string. 'It's cured with glue and ground glass. I always win the kite fights,' he said, tossing his head. 'I let my kite climb high, almost a thousand feet in the sky. I can't even see it but I rely on the vibrations of the line, and always cut the opponent's kite from the top. The trick is to release the spool rapidly and keep the line free of tangles.'

Rohini nodded. Her mother had insisted that she go to Ahmedabad with the rest of the family for the festival. Rohini wanted to stay behind in Bombay – mid-term exams and so much reading, she begged – but Harshaba would hear none of it. Now at Jag's house, on the terrace, helping his sisters string up the kites with lanterns and mending the slight tears with a sticky mixture of over-boiled rice, Rohini wished she had been more forthright with her mother. Earlier that day, while she had been introduced to Jag's cousins, his aunts and uncles and with everyone eager to talk with her, she'd forgotten her annoyance with spending two days in Ahmedabad. Now, all she sensed was irritation.

The wind picked up, and the air turned cooler. A servant brought kerosene lamps and arranged them around the terrace parapet. Jag came to Rohini at the terrace wall. 'Look,' he said, 'the kites are competing with the stars.' She looked up to where he pointed, worried by his presence so close to her. They stood quietly for a few moments watching the bright dots in the black sky. He edged closer. 'I want to tell you something that happened in South Africa. May I?'

'Oh?' she said.

Taking that as permission, he came closer, his arm barely an inch from hers. 'There was an African man, Erasmus, who worked for a company that operated the excavators in the diamond dump. His job was to sift through the diamond dust and look for residual diamonds. One evening I discovered Erasmus selling small plastic bags full of diamond bits to someone outside the gates.' Jag stared straight in the distance, as though he were talking to himself. 'I reported him to the Dutch owner of the excavation company. Erasmus was severely beaten, and then fined five thousand rand, a sum he could not pay.' Jag stopped and looked down at his hands, which were clasped tightly together. 'I began to feel guilty. I wanted to give Erasmus the money so I went to his house, driving over dirt roads through shanty townships – really just vast numbers of hovels made of corrugated iron. The poverty of the people was obvious. Just like the hutment colonies in India, except somewhat cleaner and better organized. Although the dust had a particular gritty feel. It was crusty on the lips; you could feel it at the back of your throat.' Jag cleared his throat as though reliving the dust.

'I found Erasmus, his eyes swollen shut and blood stained bandages wrapped around his arms and legs, lying senseless on a cot inside a dark one-room shack. A teenage boy who claimed to be his nephew was tending to him. I handed over the money to the boy and left.' Jag ran his hands through his hair. 'On the way back, I happened to pass a graveyard near a waste treatment plant on the outskirts of the diamond mine. I told the driver to stop the car and I walked around the graveyard. Mounds of rocks marked many of the graves, some had names scratched onto pieces of rough metal. Most had no name, just some object of affection – a cracked teapot, an old flower vase, a lopsided pinwheel. I wondered whether Erasmus would end up there because of me.' Jag's voice trembled, and for a moment Rohini thought he might break down and cry. When she glanced at him, he turned away. She wondered why he had told her about Erasmus.

ಬಿ

Rohini, Jag and his sisters set off for Patang Bazaar later that evening. Kite stalls lined the meandering alleyways. Kite sellers yelled out prices with promises of the highest, fastest, strongest kite. Music blared from somewhere. Children darted in packs from one vendor to the next.

As they approached the most crowded part of the bazaar, Jag matter-of-factly took Rohini's hand. Rohini gasped, her body stiffened. She kept walking, a half step behind Jag.

Behind them, his sisters stopped at a shop. Bits of coloured string, cigarette butts, and sweet wrappers littered the ground. Rohini's legs felt heavy, every step an effort. Her hand, the one that Jag was holding, seemed to have lost sensation; and yet . . . yet she felt the coarse bandage around his thumb, and she knew there was Mercurochrome under the bandage. She had dabbed it there herself after the kite string had cut him and left a thin stream of blood dripping over his hand and soiling his shirt. She stepped aside as he yelled for a servant to run downstairs and fetch some medicine; but the servant returned, deposited the bottle, a wad of cotton and a roll of bandage in Rohini's hands. She was left with no choice. Her own fingers shook as she tended to his injury, while he held out his hand, happy and excited by her attention.

Jag stopped at a cart where a man was removing kites from a corrugated box. Rohini stared at the box on which 'Deluxe Paints' was crossed off with a chalky substance, but the words still came through. Jag let go of her hand as he reached for his wallet. She turned and fled, melding into the crowd.

'Rohini!' Jag shouted, dropping the package of kites into the cart. Rohini quickened her pace, dodging and bumping into people. She ran through the clamour of the bazaar, all the way to the main road. She put a hand to her panting chest and when she turned Jag appeared beside her, his face full of puzzlement. 'Rohini, what happened?' He touched her elbow. 'Where are you going?'

Rohini stopped abruptly, pulled her arm away. She must tell him about Hanif. Jag would understand. He had told her about Erasmus. She tried to begin her confession. But there were no words. Only the din of the bazaar in the background.

'What's wrong?' Jag asked. 'Are you ill? Should we go home?'

Rohini nodded. She noticed his sisters coming down the lane behind him.

'Yes? Let's go then,' Jag said, concerned, but with a trace of irritation, whining like a child whose fun had been spoiled.

Chapter 10

Harshaba was eager to set a date for the engagement ceremony. Saroj had arrived from Dantali and it was a good time to plan the event. Harshaba, Motilal, Saroj and Rohini gathered on the terrace of Sagar Mahal.

A steady breeze from the Arabian Sea swept over the mansion. Two boats bobbed on the water near the shore. It was a clear day and farther towards the horizon, where the Madh peninsula jutted into the sea, the Portuguese fort was clearly visible. The beach below Sagar Mahal was empty – it was still early in the afternoon, the sun a blazing white – those who came to stroll and the boys who played cricket would emerge later, towards evening.

Rohini stood leaning against the railing, her arms outstretched. She wanted to retreat to her novels but she resigned herself to face the unwelcome subject of her matrimony once more. This is how Flaubert's heroine must have felt – hopeless and emotionally marooned.

'What's the hurry?' Motilal asked. 'The Shahs are aware that we've agreed.' He glanced uncertainly at Harshaba, knowing that ultimately whatever he said about this issue would be less important than her decision. It was a Sunday, and it was time for his nap. He heaved himself out of the chair, but when she motioned to him with her hands to stay, he sighed loudly. The seat squeaked under his weight. He trailed his hands through his thinning hair. Harshaba looked at him in irritation.

'The engagement can wait,' Saroj said. With her hair pulled in a small bun and large, intense eyes, she was taller than Rohini. She wore a starched blue sari, which only emphasized the weight she'd gained in the past few years since the birth of her two children. The boys, four and two years old, were playing with their ayah in the garden below, and as Saroj stood up to check on them she said, 'Rohini should not be distracted from her studies.'

Rohini paced the perimetre of the terrace, holding the railing with one hand, careful to avoid the splotches of pigeon droppings. She glanced appreciatively at her sister. There was a substantial age difference between them and, although they had never shared an acute intimacy, she was glad that Saroj was speaking in her defense.

'We'll have the engagement next month,' Harshaba announced.

Rohini stopped pacing. She stood speechless, facing the sea, her back towards the others. The waves were receding, leaving the sand strewn with parched seaweed. The two boats had hoisted their sails and were moving towards the horizon.

'What?' Saroj said. 'Next month?'

Saroj had been married soon after her fourteenth birthday. Her husband, Nalin, who was twenty at that time, belonged to an upper-class family of mill-owners in Dantali, a small town near Ahmedabad. Motilal and Harshaba knew that Nalin was the most eligible man in all of Gujarat, a prospect not to be passed up at any cost, and Saroj didn't question her parents' choice.

In Dantali there wasn't much – three temples, a government-run school, a few small shops around the clock tower, a cinema, a dispensary, and a library. Nalin's family owned a large house on the outskirts, surrounded by *kamrakh* trees on one side, and fields with dancing peacocks on the other. It was a slow, pastoral life, and Saroj was treated like a princess. Whenever she wished to go anywhere, the *ghoda-gadi* with two white horses, a brass-trimmed carriage, attended by a coachman and a footman, was summoned from the stables.

Her household duties were minimal. There were servants and cooks and gardeners to look after the house. Nalin left for the mills early each morning and returned well after sundown. On Sundays he would sprawl out on a divan in the balcony, the radio by his head, and, to the slow droning of cricket commentary, fall asleep with his mouth open.

Saroj's father-in-law attended the mills every morning, returned at lunchtime, and then vanished to some part of the house for the rest of the day. Her mother-in-law usually kept to herself, except on those evenings when she suddenly summoned the carriage and asked to be taken into town. On such occasions, she would wander aimlessly for a while, and then return home as suddenly as she had departed. For several years before Saroj's children were born, she felt as though she lived alone in the big house.

Saroj filled her days reading books in Gujarati borrowed from the library, which was a one-room building in the centre of town, and open for two hours every day, except

Sunday and public holidays. Saroj was a regular visitor. Sometimes an elderly couple stopped by for the newspaper, or a few giggling schoolchildren bored with playing on the footpaths. The librarian, a stooped man, shuffled around, randomly removing books from the shelves and putting them back. He would smile broadly at Saroj, and then scurry over to his desk to wait patiently until she made her selection. Each time he would check her library card, and with great effort, squinting and pointing at each letter, copy the titles of her books.

Saroj read about the Indus Valley civilization, the dynasties of the Mauryas and the Moghuls. She read books on Hinduism and biographies of the great saints, English dramas and collections of short stories. Sometimes the library received American magazines donated by missionaries, and in these Saroj read about scientific discoveries and popular inventions. But there was no one to discuss the books with, no one to endorse or refute the views she stumbled on, or share the thrill of her knowledge of the ways of the world.

Nalin's older brother was married to a Swedish woman and they lived near Stockholm. No one seemed to recall the Swedish woman's name – she was referred to simply as 'Swedish'. Once, during their visit to India, Swedish said to Saroj, 'We live in a small town called Västervik. It is like Dantali. You should come.' For a while Saroj was swept up in the romance of it all – of travelling by steamer to a foreign land, strolling along lamplit promenades, looking into exotic shops, and dining by candlelight in fine hotels – scenes she had read about in the library books – but when she broached the subject with Nalin, he grunted dismissively, so she went back to her lonely, tedious routine. Her husband was intelligent, but dull and sullen, and his newly acquired habit of smoking cigarettes aggravated his sullenness. She learned to accept his odd personality and in so doing began resenting her parents, who, it was becoming obvious to her, had deprived her of the opportunity of a formal education and a more interesting life.

On the terrace at Sagar Mahal, Rohini turned to her mother, 'How can I marry him after one or two meetings? We need more time.'

Harshaba looked her up and down. 'I'm going to my room,' she said quietly. She gestured to Motilal and he followed her out.

'Don't worry,' Saroj said to Rohini, 'I'll talk to her later.'

Rohini crossed the terrace and sank into her father's chair. She stared at Saroj for a moment. 'What if ... there's someone else? What if I like ...' She looked away, her heart beating fast.

Saroj leaned into the cushions, tucked one leg under her. 'After marriage you learn to like your husband. You adjust.'

'Adjust?'

'Yes, you adjust to everything,' Saroj said quietly. 'When I was married, I didn't even know how to talk to him. I would think a hundred times before uttering a line. For the first few months he didn't even know I existed, except ... oh, never mind.' Saroj looked away as she recalled Nalin's polite nightly knocks on her bedroom door in Dantali. Quickly and quietly he would slip under the sheets, and then just as quickly and quietly he would be done with her and return to his room next door. In the morning when she tried to read some emotion on his face, he offered only a blunt nod before leaving for the mills. She said to Rohini, 'We lived in the same house, but we went for days without talking because there was nothing to say.'

'And now?'

'Now,' Saroj tried to smile. 'I have children,' she said with a shrug.

'Your boys are wonderful, although rather mischievous,' Rohini laughed lightly. 'But you marrying a stranger . . . I could never do that.'

'You don't have to do that,' Saroj said. 'You're a college girl! I heard that you and Jagmohan talked about history and literature. You made quite an impression on him. "Rohini is beautiful *and* intelligent," he was telling everyone in Ahmedabad. I was so happy to hear that. You have a better understanding of the world than I do.' Saroj laughed. 'I should be coming to you for advice.'

'At college . . .' Rohini started, the fear in her voice mixed with hope. 'At college, I've made some friends . . .' It was right at the surface, the need to divulge the bold desires of her heart to her big sister, who could surely make everything right. 'I want to . . . what do you think of . . .?'

'What do I think of Jagmohan?' Saroj said brightly. She leaned towards Rohini and took her hand. 'He's perfect for you,' she said, squeezing Rohini's hand. Momentarily, Rohini held Saroj's gaze and when she lowered her eyes, Saroj mistook the gesture for shyness.

Chapter 11

At Café Royal, Hanif and Pervez were talking about America as they waited for Rohini – more accurately, Pervez was talking and his friend was feigning interest – and when she approached their table, Pervez missed the moment when Hanif's eyes met hers, the wordless conversation that bespoke countless lines of longing.

'Have you ordered something?' Rohini said as she sat down.

'We were waiting for you,' Hanif said. 'Pervez is going to America.'

'America? Really?' Rohini said.

Pervez laughed. 'Nothing is definite. My father wants to send me for further studies.'

'My brother,' Rohini said, 'is going to America as well. Your father and mine met last week to discuss some business issues – I know my father wants to export silk. In any case, your father must have talked about America and convinced my father to send Mahesh.'

'No one talked to my father about sending me to America,' Hanif said.

They ordered samosas with the tea and when the plates came, they ate hungrily. How easy and lighthearted she felt around Hanif. Still, there was no avoiding the reality of her impending engagement; images from Ahmedabad rose like misshapen bubbles from time to time.

Hanif was in high spirits. The All India Radio competition was three months away. 'I'm practicing like a mad person,' he said.

'You'll win,' Rohini said. 'I'm sure of it.'

Hanif smiled broadly. If he won, he would be assured a recording contract.

The lunch hour flew by. Hanif had to return to the office. She stood, and felt his arm brush against hers. They stood close, facing each other. She needed to tell him about Jag and the potential engagement. Instead, she said, 'There's a new picture at Bandra Talkies.'

'Yes, I know,' he said. 'Sunday?' He nodded and smiled as he left.

Rohini waited with Pervez while he finished his tea.

Suddenly there was a loud commotion outside. Pervez gulped his tea and they hurried to the entrance to see what it was. A procession of men and women carrying signs and banners was marching down the road. Traffic had come to a standstill. A man at the front carried a megaphone and the crowd behind him echoed the slogans he shouted: 'Land to the tiller! Out with the foreign-imperialist-capitalist! The nation's wealth in the nation's hands! Social equality for women! Social justice for untouchables!' Young men with handkerchiefs tied around their heads punched their fists in the air as they yelled. Policemen brandishing long sticks patrolled the edge of the procession, blowing whistles to keep order.

'It's the Communist Party,' Pervez said turning to Rohini. 'Their ideas are conservative and ineffective,' he muttered. 'They have no national spirit.'

'No national spirit? Look at them, they have energy and courage . . .'

Pervez cut her off. 'They're showing frustration, that's all. Nothing will come of this.'

Rohini remained focused on the stream of humanity marching past. There was no mistaking the conviction in their cries. She wanted to run outside and join in their revolt. Behind her the clinking of cups and plates being cleared grew louder. Outside the crowd thinned and Rohini noticed Hanif on the other side of the road. He had been caught in the chaos on leaving the cafe. Now he was walking hurriedly in the direction of the train station. Emboldened by the communist march, and, prompted by the sight of Hanif in the distance, she turned to Pervez. In a low, urgent voice she said, 'My parents have arranged my marriage to a man in Ahmedabad . . .' Pervez wasn't listening.

'Marxism,' he said to her. 'Marxism is taking hold in Calcutta. The CPI is a powerful party. I think a communist revolution is likely in India.'

'A communist revolution,' she said, turning away in frustration.

Chapter 12

After reading a book about business and free enterprise, Mahesh determined that the family needed to diversify; it was too reliant on silk and the war had shown how ingenuity could find alternatives when silk was in scarce supply. He had read an article about petrochemicals, but oil was not something India possessed in vast quantities. So he looked around for something else in abundance and found it right in front of his eyes. The sea. He worked quietly in his room for days, coming down only for meals, and then approached Motilal with his plan.

'The sea at Versova is rich in prawns and bummalo,' Mahesh said excitedly to his father. 'We start with two fishing trawlers. After the initial investment, we buy two more.'

Mahesh had the same high forehead and straight nose as Motilal. He was tall and muscular – every morning, in sports shorts and canvas shoes, no shirt, he sprinted the beach all the way to the Versova-Juhu quicksand. On the way back he threw kicks in the air and grappled with an imaginary opponent, imitating the jujitsu moves he'd seen in a silent Japanese film.

'Trawlers?' Motilal asked. 'There's already a fishing village at Versova.'

'But that's exactly the point,' Mahesh said, and explained that while the fishermen were using small fishing boats, his plan was to employ a modern vessel with a double rig, motorized winch, and sonar system. And the fishermen were already there to employ. 'Gradually we take over the entire fishing industry along the western coast.'

Motilal did not dismiss the plan, said he wanted time to think about it, and suggested that Mahesh discuss it with Shrikant. Since it didn't require much capital, Motilal thought it would be good for his sons to embark on something together.

Shrikant, taller than Mahesh, and eight years older, was thin and bony. The Bell's palsy he'd suffered as a child had marred his lower jaw, and he'd developed the self-conscious habit of turning his head to hide the affected side. He listened attentively as Mahesh explained the project. 'We'll call it Chimanji Brothers Fishing Company,' he said to Mahesh, and over the next few weeks helped Mahesh procure licenses, consult solicitors and interview workers. He accompanied Mahesh to Kerala to purchase two trawlers.

On the day the trawlers were to be launched, when Mahesh came down for morning tea, Shrikant was already there, slouched in a chair and absently swirling the spoon in the sugar bowl. The newspapers lay folded on the table beside the tea tray. Mahesh whistled as he settled down at the table with his tea and the paper.

'We can't launch the trawlers,' Shrikant said, quietly. 'We must cancel everything. This fishing business is not for us. People will call us fisherfolk. It'll be disgraceful.'

'Nobody will say anything.' Mahesh slurped his tea. 'And why should we care?'

'Mahesh, let me remind you that we're Hindus, and we don't believe in killing anything. I've decided, we're not going to launch those trawlers.'

Mahesh set his teacup down with a loud clatter.

'You'll be going away to America,' Shrikant said, with icy reproach. 'Or have you decided not to go now?'

'Of course I'm going to America,' Mahesh said. 'But I'll be back in a few years. Until then, you run the show. You can manage, can't you?'

Shrikant grunted and folded his arms across his chest. 'Do you know how hard our forefathers worked to build the family's reputation? Do you? It's our responsibility to uphold the family name.'

Mahesh stared at Shrikant. He understood that the family's reputation was paramount. 'But, wait,' he said. 'Our forefathers, you say? Have you forgotten?'

'What? I haven't forgotten anything!'

'As I recall,' Mahesh cut in, 'our forefathers weren't exactly the most honourable businessmen themselves.'

'Look, don't bring up the past and don't make excuses. We're not getting involved with fishing, and that's the end of the story.'

Mahesh looked around the room. 'We must do it!' he said, raising his voice and stomping one foot on the floor. Shrikant shrugged dismissively. Mahesh stood up and flung the newspaper across the dining room, narrowly missing Motilal at the door. Shrikant explained the situation to their father – over Mahesh's angry interjections.

Motilal looked from one son to the other. He admired Mahesh's zeal. But Shrikant was right. Killing fish was wrong. The family name would be disgraced forever. They would go down in the annals of history not as reputed silk merchants, but as fishermen. Fishermen! What a thought. 'Shrikant is right,' Motilal said slowly. 'We have to remember who we are. Besides, I have to think about Rohini. What will the Shahs say if we tell them we are now in the fish business? They in diamonds, and we in fish! And there's Sumitra and Amrita still to be married. And you, Mahesh – who will marry you?' Motilal pointed a hand at Mahesh's face. 'Which father will give their daughter to a fisherman?'

Mahesh opened and closed his mouth and wiped the sweat from his forehead with his hand. Motilal gathered up the newspaper and left the room. Shrikant turned his head, but Mahesh saw the small smug smile on his face. He threw an irritated look at Shrikant and stormed out to the verandah to glare at the sea.

He was more furious than he remembered ever having been before. The Chimanji Brothers Fishing Company folded before it started – all for the sake of the family's reputation.

Chapter 13

Rohini stood at the compound wall facing the sea, her sari filling with the wind, and strands of hair brushing her face. The sun, weak and dim behind thick clouds, would be setting soon. She trained her eyes to the waves and watched them rising and rolling. To become Jag's wife . . . his house in Ahmedabad, his sisters, his parents, sharing her days with him, and her nights . . . but she could only imagine Hanif's embrace. If she married Jag, could she clandestinely journey to Bombay each month to see Hanif? Like Emma Bovary? Those things happened only in novels, and that too, only in Europe or America, not in India. Jag said he wanted to show her the game parks in Africa, and take her to Cape Town and up the coast to Durban. It would be an exotic life. And yet . . . the casual brush of Hanif's shoulder, the press of his hand, his jokes – these had become such overwhelming joys. She pictured Hanif sitting before the harmonium . . . was he singing a new ghazal? But . . . her desire wasn't worth the suffering it would cause her family. Forbearance was a virtue. Blankness nudged her senses. In the distance the hounding waves raged taller and whiter.

Rohini trudged back to the house. She would tell him tomorrow. She would be firm, no matter what he said. Late that night after her sisters were asleep she opened the armoire. Behind the stacks of saris and petticoats there were eleven small bundles. She reread all the letters to make sure there wasn't a word or a line she had failed to notice before, and then looked through the brown envelope filled with stubs of cinema tickets, remembering the evening but not the movie.

ฑ฿

At Churchgate station, Rohini and Hanif walked towards a bench at the end of platform five, where the last train car stopped. Hanif bought two bottles of cold lemon drink from the kiosk and after they sat down he finished his drink quickly while she held her bottle with both hands. Two small beggar children, a boy and a girl, were huddled in a corner next to the crates at the kiosk. They were shovelling handfuls of rice into their mouths from one aluminum bowl balanced between them. Reading the anxiety on Rohini's face Hanif asked what was wrong. She kept staring at the ground. Two trains came and went. On the opposite platform a man in a business suit and a briefcase drew on his cigarette and then tossed the butt onto the tracks where it lay amongst other bits of garbage – crumpled wrappers, bottle caps, and ticket stubs. The two children finished their bowl of rice. The boy got up and left; the girl stayed huddled beside the crates.

Rohini sighed and stammered through the words: 'My parents . . . are . . . planning my engagement . . .' She stared at her lap, her shoulders hunched in distress. 'We can't . . . meet . . . anymore. And please, don't send any letters with

Pervez.' She glanced at him and couldn't bear his tormented face. Tears welled in her eyes and the rest of her words were broken by sobs. 'I've decided to marry the man they've chosen. It is my duty. Please, do you . . . can you . . . understand?'

'Yes, I understand,' he whispered, but he did not understand at all. He stared at her, his teeth clamped over his lower lip. Her words tolled randomly in his thoughts – parents-engagement-duty-letters – and the image of her crying wrung his heart with a malicious energy he didn't know existed in the world.

A train swept in with a startling whistle. With shaking hands Rohini thrust her unfinished lemon drink at Hanif and cast a deep, forlorn look at his face. He accepted the bottle as though it was a precious parting gift and watched her wipe her hands on her sari. Then she was gone.

Hanif sat on the bench staring at the train tracks, elbows on his knees, and a lemon drink bottle in each hand. He felt the ground rumble each time another train approached and the damp rush of air that filled his shirt carried the foul smell of coal and grease.

When he finally walked back to the kiosk to return the bottles, the small girl was still there, hunched near the counter. She reached for the bottles, set the empty one on the ground beside her, and put the full one to her lips, her eyes brightening at the sweetness. Hanif watched her, resenting her simple contentment.

Chapter 14

Streams of yellow and orange marigolds decorated the gate of Jag's house. Moist, red rose petals lay scattered along the stone pathway that led to the front door. When Rohini arrived with her family, the guests were already in the back garden, seated under a large tent, the *shamiana*, specially constructed for the engagement ceremony. The morning breeze that rustled the leaves of the fig trees felt warm and arid. 'The hot season has come early this year,' the ladies under the shamiana said to each other, dabbing their necks with embroidered handkerchiefs.

Rohini looked down at her gold and white sari that felt stiff and weighty, and twisted the gold bangles on her wrists. A black marble Ganesh sat in the center of the low stage constructed at the far end of the shamiana. Six low stools – three on either side – covered with small silk mats, had been placed before an assortment of colourful objects for the ceremony – flowers, bowls of red powder, oil lamps, incense sticks and fruits. The pujari in a white dhoti, his bare upper body exposing the holy thread worn diagonally across his chest, tinkered with the objects on the stage, making sure nothing had been forgotten.

Next to the stage, three musicians had already started

playing. Rohini glanced at the *shehnai* – at its wooden fluted body and brass cone – and the shehnai player – his eyes closed in concentration, his cheeks puffed full as he blew into the reed, his body swaying to the rhythm. The tabla player, a young boy of fourteen or fifteen, was nodding and beating his fingers with gusto. She averted her eyes the moment she noticed the third instrument, but her face clouded. She forced herself to focus on the shehnai and tabla and ignore the delicate insistent musings of the harmonium.

On stage, Rohini sat between her parents, Jag directly across from her. She stared at the paraphernalia on the floor between them. When the pujari began the Ganesh puja, Rohini tried to pay attention. The words sounded doom-filled and decisive. She glanced at Jag and found him looking directly at her. The joy on his face was clear, pure. She wished she could be as certain as him. Could he read the reluctance in her eyes? She looked away.

The puja's drone seemed endless. She looked at the black Ganesh statue, serene and demure, exuding calmness. Her gaze fell on Ganesh's elephant trunk that swirled playfully upward and imagined another man waiting for her at the newspaper kiosk on platform five, outside Princess Kulfi House, near the horse-and-buggy stand at Apollo Bunder . . . such bright, happy, persistent images of him.

Jag's mother spread a white cloth and laid a tray with a mixture of water and *kankoo* before Rohini. Rohini lifted her sari to her ankles and dipped her feet in the red liquid. The redness came up between her toes, unevenly colouring her feet. Removing her feet one at a time from the tray, she pressed them onto the cloth. Motilal offered the coconut to

Jag's parents and, along with it, the customary one-rupee note and twenty-five-paisa coin.

Rohini accepted her gifts – velvet-covered cases of jewellery and boxes of saris – and bowed to Jag's parents. She was going through the actions without enthusiasm, but also without remorse. When Jag's mother slipped a ring on Rohini's finger she stared at it blankly. She was reminded of the diamond miner whom Jag had encountered in South Africa. What was his name? She saw the man, beaten and senseless. Erasmus. She hoped Erasmus was still alive.

After the ceremony, Jag circulated among the guests, radiant and confident. Rohini stayed by his side. Jag kept glancing openly at her, touching her elbow as he introduced her to his relatives. He hugged his friends and acknowledged their congratulations with a wide grin. The tables were laden with food, but she had no appetite. She put on a conciliatory smile as Jag deposited a bowl of sweets into her hands. She could no longer ignore the heat, which now seemed to her to be a burning malevolence. Jag's sisters offered to take her inside the house where she could sit under a fan, but she said weakly, 'I'm okay, I'll endure it.'

The guests left jovial and tired and the place buzzed for a while with the activity of house servants cleaning up. Rohini watched the gardener from the sitting room window sweeping petals off the walkway. She was now officially engaged to Jag. The house echoed to the sound of a servant throwing the bolt on an outside door.

III

INDEPENDENCE

Chapter 15

Hanif and Pervez walked in silence from the bus stand to Hanif's house. The evening sky stretched dull and colourless. Hanif loosened his tie and undid the top shirt button. His black shoes, polished that morning before work, were covered with a thin layer of dust.

Hanif kept thinking about Rohini. Her parting words had drained all the confidence out of him and, like an unfair verdict, made him feel demoralized and small. The reality of rejection hammered his heart; he hadn't felt like going to work; he stopped preparing for the music competition. Each night he had opened the Koran and turned the pages feverishly in the hope of finding a prescription for his melancholy.

'Come in,' Hanif said to Pervez, fishing for a key in his pocket. The house was dark and quiet. Hanif's mother was away in Surat for a week and his father was still at the office. 'Go to the music room, I'll come in a minute,' Hanif said. He left his briefcase on a chair in the hall, and after splashing his face with water in the bathroom, joined Pervez in the music room. He opened the windows but didn't bother with the stops; there didn't seem to be a breeze anyway. Slumped down on his knees before the harmonium, he lifted the cloth cover and unhooked the clasps. For a moment he stared at the keys as though he'd completely forgotten what to do with them.

'Well, what did she say?' Pervez asked, settling into an armchair.

'What does it matter?' Hanif's fingers scaled the keys randomly.

'You can't just sit here playing the harmonium,' Pervez said. 'Do something!' Pervez had anticipated this break-up all along – had he not warned Hanif repeatedly? – but he couldn't bear to see his friend in this hopeless state.

'Do what? Tell me, what should I do?' Over slow, lonely notes, Hanif's thoughts went to the platform at Churchgate. *I've decided to marry the person they've chosen.* He had wanted to shout at her, *What about me? Do I count for nothing?* Was he now supposed to forget the chuum-chuum of her anklets, the *kajol* that highlighted her eyes, and the jasmine scent that lived around her? What of the countless hours they'd spent together, at Café Royal, at cinema houses . . . the countless nights he'd stayed up composing poems for her? How easily she had dismissed him! She was doing what her parents wanted, but, clearly, she was also choosing the easier, more comfortable life, a life among her own people. He was disgusted at how she had led him on, pretending to be taken by his music, his voice, disgusted at how she had failed to comprehend the unstated bond between them. Yet . . . he couldn't stop thinking about the arresting beauty of her face, the softness of her hands, the way she looked shyly at him.

Was there something he could do to get her back? He looked blankly at Pervez, who crossed his arms over his chest and turned away; he had no time for matters of the heart.

Hanif played the harmonium, the notes low and dismal, devoid of rhythm. A crow settled on the ledge at the window, craned its neck to peek inside, and then without fully spreading its wings, leapt off the ledge and disappeared. From the neighbour's kitchen came the clang of pots and pans and voices talking excitedly.

'There's nothing you can do,' Pervez said. 'Come, play something properly.'

Hanif began the ghazal he had known since childhood, the one written by Bahadur Shah.

> My life's without a ray of light,
> It brings no solace to heart or eye;
> Out of dust, and to dust again,
> I'm of little use to anyone; let me say goodbye.

As he sang the Urdu words, the emperor's lament punctuated his own sadness.

૭૦

From the music room Iqbalji's voice could be heard over Hanif's singing, 'Come on, take a breath at the right time, between the beats, don't wait'; 'Higher, higher, don't be lazy, you must build your range'; 'No, don't strain like that, make it effortless'; '*Listen* to the notes . . . you must train your ears, not just your voice.'

Iqbalji's sparse, grey hair was parted at the side and he wore loose fitting beige trousers and a white shirt. A gold chain from a pocket watch dangled from his belt loop. When he was nineteen his self-trained baritone voice had landed him a job in the film industry, but that same year he won a scholarship to read economics at Oxford. Excited at the prospect of travelling abroad, he had given up his music career for England. Now, since he had a family to support, he worked for a British trading firm in Bombay, his love for music channeled into coaching young promising ghazal singers like Hanif. At their first meeting, when Hanif had tried to ask about his fees, Iqbalji had waved the question away and said, 'Have you heard of Mirza Ghalib? He was a *great* Urdu poet. His lyrical coherence and his sense of artistry were unbelievable. He was a true genius.'

Hanif had nodded and asked, 'And Faiz, another great, no? I like his polished style and diction. About our lessons and the money . . .'

'Faiz was good,' Iqbalji interjected, 'but Ghalib's corpus of poetry is much bigger and more refined. *He* influenced Faiz, did you know? The title of Faiz's first work, *Naqsh-e-Faryadi*, comes straight from a ghazal by Ghalib.'

During the practice session that evening, Iqbalji clicked his tongue and threw his hands in the air. 'You're wasting my time, Hanif. What's happened to you?' he shouted. 'Whatever it is, something at the office, a stupid girl . . . you have to put everything else aside. Understand?'

Hanif nodded.

The next day Iqbalji arrived at Hanif's house with a small attaché case, which, despite its handles, he clutched tightly under his arm. Instead of sitting on the floor before the harmonium, Iqbalji went to a chair and motioned for Hanif to sit in the chair next to him. From the attaché he pulled out a file of yellowed newspaper cuttings.

One by one he showed Hanif the articles from the London papers: *Caruso performs at Covent Gardens; The man from Naples with a voice of gold; Caruso in Verdi's* Aida; *Caruso in* Il Travatore; *Caruso sings in Puccini's* Tosca; *The greatest tenor of the 20th century; Caruso in America, performs in Metropolitan.*

Hanif glanced at the cuttings and listened to Iqbalji with mild curiosity. He shifted uneasily in his chair, eyeing the harmonium on the floor with the blue cover still on.

Iqbalji gathered the newspaper clippings and replaced the file in his attaché case. 'Now you will hear his voice,' he said, pulling out two 78-rpm records. Gesturing towards the record player he handed the bulky discs to Hanif. 'Puccini, yes, this one first please, then, Verdi.' Iqbalji rose to close the door and windows, and then hurried to the chair to settle down with a sigh. Hanif prepared the record player, toggling the wall switch until the red power light came on. Two years ago they'd sold the Victrola hand-crank phonograph that his parents had bought when they were married, and replaced it with this new HMV model that had a teakwood housing for the speakers, chrome knobs, and a transparent plastic cover.

Hanif bent down and lifted the arm of the player, blew lightly to get the dust off the needle, and placed it gently on the record.

The sounds of the orchestra, and Caruso's brave voice, low at first, then tempered and melancholic filled the room . . . it was Rudolfo's famous aria from *La Bohème* . . .

Che gelida manina,
se la lasci riscaldar.
Cercar che giova?
Al buio non si trova.
Ma per fortuna
è una notte di luna,
e qui la luna
l'abbiamo vicina . . .

Hanif didn't understand the words and he was certain that Iqbalji could only have given him a rough translation because he knew the storyline, but soon he stopped fidgeting and was spellbound.

'His voice is incredible!' Hanif said as the record ended and he rose to tend to the player.

Iqbalji smiled. 'Caruso's vocal chords were in the heart muscle rather than the larynx.'

'Really? Is that possible?'

'Well, that's what I read,' Iqbalji said. 'But the excessive pressure eventually wore down his diaphragm and lungs. Come, let's have the next one.' Iqbalji crossed one leg over the other and closed his eyes. After changing the record, Hanif leaned back in the chair and did the same. 'It can move the soul,' Iqbalji whispered, as Verdi came on . . . his most famous tenor aria, with Caruso as Radamès in *Aida* . . .

Se quel guerrier?
Io fossi! se il mio sogno?
S'avverasse! . . . Un esercito di prodi?
Da me guidato . . . e la vittoria . . . e il plauso?
Di Menfi tutta! E a te, mia dolce Aida?
Tornar di lauri cinto . . .

They listened in silence until the recording ended. As Hanif rose to turn off the player, Iqbalji said, 'The solo arias, the duets and the choruses are fully integrated into the dramatic flow. But sometimes there's not even a plausible story, it's all about the sound and the spectacle.'

Hanif started composing his own ghazals, short lyrics in Urdu or Hindi that he hummed on the train to work. In the evenings when he sat with the harmonium trying out different sequences, he set the words to a melody and wrote the verses in a notebook. He'd never paid much attention to the structure of the ghazal before — five to fifteen couplets, of equal length and metre, a refrain at the end of both lines of the first couplet; each verse, a complete unit, a poem in itself. The final couplet, the poet's signature, was a self-reference rendering a direct, intense declaration of feeling.

Composing took time and although he was constantly tearing out pages of the notebook, it further concentrated his musical artistry. He grew aware of the range of emotions that could be conjured in a single word. He knew that music was a conglomeration of sound and sense, and it could be perfected with commitment and discipline. But now he felt he was moving beyond mere proficiency and skill into a place he could neither describe nor explain. The collection of ghazals that grew in his notebook was unforced and openhearted. His best ghazals, by far the most evocative, in which he bared his soul, focused on failed hopes and unrequited love.

ೞ

Hanif checked himself in the well-lit dressing room mirror. He looked regal in the white and gold sherwani he'd purchased for the competition. Humming and rotating his wrists, he paced the dressing room. He took a few sips of tepid water from the flask he had brought from home. 'The vocal chords must be kept limber,' Iqbalji had warned. 'Don't drink anything too hot or too cold.'

On stage, Hanif bowed to the audience, then to the harmonium. After settling himself at the instrument, he adjusted the knobs, intermittently flexing his fingers, playing a few notes and turning the knobs again. 'Don't be in a hurry to start,' Iqbalji had advised. Finally, he nodded to the accompanists on sitar, tabla and tanpura seated on the floor in a semi-circle to his right. The audience grew quiet as the notes of the harmonium and the other instruments spread over the auditorium. Then came Hanif's voice. It was the ghazal he had known since childhood, written by Bahadur Shah Zafar.

> I feel ill at ease with such wasted health;
> Who in this world has sensed peace and mirth?
> The nightingale weeps, to hunter and gardener,
> 'Imprisonment's our lot, upon this earth.'

Hanif worried about the lights in the auditorium – too bright or too dim, he couldn't decide . . .

> Tell these emotions to dwell elsewhere;
> There's no room for them in this besmirched heart.

He worried about a twitch that suddenly developed at his eye; he worried about the harmonium being out of tune . . .

I had begged for a life, four days in length;
Two days have passed in pining, and two in wait;
I must be wretched, for even two yards
Were hard to find in my beloved State.

The applause at the end of the song startled Hanif and for a moment he looked at the audience as though he'd forgotten they were there. He breathed deeply before beginning the second song. The air smelled faintly of new varnish. The mood of the event – both festive and tension-filled – that had made him uneasy a few minutes ago, now suddenly inspired him. His mind wandered to recording studios and contracts with radio stations, to performances in Delhi and Calcutta. He thought of Caruso, the Italian, and wondered whether he had ever heard a ghazal. He closed his eyes and concentrated on the tabla. *Dhin-taka-dhin.* The notes from the harmonium melded gently with his voice. The audience grew still. He sang some ghazals by Ghalib and Faiz, one by Raaz Allahbadi, and an old favourite by Fayyaz Hashmi – *Aaj Janee Ki Zid Na Karo.*

Before singing the last ghazal and, as his fingers scaled the keyboard, Hanif looked towards the judges. Perspiration dotted his forehead; he longed to shift his knees and stretch his legs. *Raatein Thi Chandni*, 'this moon-soaked night', a song about a bee and a flower, was his own composition. His voice carried the words with sincerity and passion. His face grew rapturous, as though he were seeing the bumblebee and the flower he sang about. At the high notes, while the audience held their breath, his voice held the melody effortlessly. Even Iqbalji, sitting in the back row, had never heard him sing with such verve and abandon. When the song ended, and, as Hanif's voice faded to the final thump of the tabla and the quiet, melancholic reverberation of the harmonium, the audience was on its feet, the ovation louder than a monsoon downpour.

A slow, tired smile stretched on Hanif's face. He felt as light as the seagulls that swooped around Chowpatty Beach. He gave in to the crowd, to their clapping and cheering, and submitted to the glory of the moment.

Then, without warning, the smile disappeared from his face. He reached in the pocket of his sherwani for a handkerchief and dabbed his forehead. The applause continued, but now the sound fell around him, empty and distant. Gone were his thoughts of fame and grandeur, of concerts and recording contracts. Instead, his mind filled with the cheerless, dismal realization that he had lost Rohini. As he closed the harmonium his face grew serious and still. He bowed to the audience, thanked the accompanists, and fled backstage. When the results were announced, he accepted the winner's bouquet without joy, without excitement.

Chapter 16

On the final day of the cricket Test match against England, monsoon clouds brooded over Bombay. It was hardly a promising morning for any activity, but with much difficulty Iqbalji had procured two tickets and invited Hanif to join him. Hanif wasn't a cricket fan, but from radio commentary and office chatter he knew that the Australian team had recently humiliated India, that Vijay Hazrath was India's top batsman, and that Lala Amarnath was everyone's favourite bowler.

'Let's pray the rain holds off,' Iqbalji said, glancing at the heavy sky and tightening his grip on the wooden handle of his umbrella as they arrived at the stadium.

An usher directed them to their seats in the clubhouse and Hanif was surprised. The area under the awning was reserved for the British and upper-class Indians; he had expected to sit in the lower stalls. Noticing Iqbalji's smart beige trousers and shirt with cufflinks, Hanif looked down self-consciously at his own clothes.

Two days ago India had won the toss. The scoreboard now read: India 241, England 235. India was batting again. But in less than an hour, four players including the captain were caught out. 'There's still a chance,' Hanif said, looking up at the slightly clearing sky as if it were an omen. Another Indian player stumbled attempting a quick single and the wicket-keeper swept off the bails. A mighty groan of dismay rose from the packed stands.

Hanif found himself cheering when Vijay Hazrath strutted onto the field, his bat poised jauntily on his shoulder, and hit his first ball into the stands for a six. However with the next ball, he struck his pads and the umpire called leg before wicket. Hazrath was out for a score of just six. India's chances were all but dashed. Within minutes, three more batsmen were bowled by the Englishmen and England, coming in at 235, had a mere 290 runs to beat. It was a sorry day for Indian cricket, was the murmured consensus.

The umpires called lunch and subdued fans shuffled from their seats. 'We can get something there,' Hanif said, pointing to the dozens of food carts lined up on the footpaths behind the stands. Iqbalji grunted and followed Hanif; now that India looked set to lose, he didn't care about lunch. They watched the bhelpuri-walla dip a used plate in a bucket of murky water, swish it around, and hand it to the next customer. Iqbalji turned to Hanif. 'In the Indian edition of the Oxford Dictionary,' he said, 'the word "hygiene" is left out.'

'But this is the tastiest food,' Hanif laughed. 'Makes the stomach strong.'

After lunch, with England batting, it started to drizzle and the red ball moved erratically when it came off the pitch, robbing India's bowlers of control and leaving their captain's strategy of a brutal attack in tatters; the English batsmen kept knocking it to the boundary. A heartrending groan accompanied the umpire's raising of his right arm into the air to signal four runs to the scoreboard. By the four o'clock tea-break, England was 287 for only five wickets, with five batsmen left to play and only fourteen runs needed.

After tea and finger sandwiches at the snack bar, Iqbalji and Hanif looked for the toilets, which were down a long corridor and past a wood-panelled foyer. A round table with an arrangement of red and white roses decorated the centre of the foyer. Two doors, marked 'ladies' and 'gents' in shiny, brass lettering stood on the far side.

Inside the gents' room was a lounge with sofas and chairs, magazines and cigars. The toilets were clean and dry; there were shell shaped dishes of soap at the marble sinks and white towels in assorted sizes. The attendant, a dark, burly man, brought out a bottle of *eau de cologne* and offered to freshen their handkerchiefs when Iqbaliji slipped him a few coins. Hanif was rather enjoying himself; the day with his music teacher was turning out to be better than he'd expected. It would be more fun if India were winning, but still, they could always blame the weather.

As they emerged from the gents' lounge Hanif froze. There, next to the big vase of red and white roses in a purple sari – Rohini, talking with another man and woman, both finely dressed. Hanif felt weak at the knees. He wanted to turn and walk back into the gents' lounge, go to the marble sink and wash his hands again. But he stood in the doorway unable to take his eyes off of her.

Her gaze met his, and he saw recognition leaping into her eyes.

'You know them?' Iqbalji asked Hanif.

Hanif nodded, his eyes focused on Rohini.

It was Saroj and her husband, Nalin, with Rohini.

'Good afternoon. I'm Hanif Wali Hussein,' he said, walking towards them. He was surprised at himself, and instantly wished he'd kept quiet. 'And this is Mr Iqbalji. He's a member of the club. He studied in England. Oxford. He's a musician, you see. Cricket. He likes cricket. And I like cricket, too.' He was babbling and he knew it, but he couldn't help himself. 'I work for a radio station. All India Radio.' He looked at Rohini. 'From college. Uh, we met in college. And music. Yes. College,' he stammered.

'Ah, yes, from college,' Saroj said, smiling politely. 'I'm Rohini's sister.'

'Nalin. I'm Rohini's brother-in-law. Delighted to meet you,' Nalin said, bowing slightly.

Iqbalji nodded.

Hanif's eyes hadn't left Rohini's face.

Rohini focused on the roses and noticed that there were more red ones than white ones. In one fist she crimped the corner of her sari, and with her thumb she twirled her diamond-encrusted engagement ring.

Only a few days ago she'd locked her bedroom door, brought out the silken bundles, and read Hanif's letters. She had heard his voice pronouncing the words in perfect Urdu diction. Small endearing details about him – the dense curly hair on his arm flattened at the wrist where he wore his watch, the directness with which he'd often told her, 'Even when you frown, you are beautiful' – crept into her thoughts as she finished one letter and took up another. When she completed reading them all, she decided to get rid of the letters. She'd stuffed them in her book bag and planned to dispose them in the rubbish bin at college. But when she got there a large crowd was clamouring outside the gates, which were barricaded with wooden crates. She saw police gathering by the edges of the crowd. Gandhiji was in Bombay to meet with leading Indian industrialists and people were protesting about his disregard for poor peasants. Classes were cancelled that day and she had stood watching the protest from a safe distance for a few minutes before leaving, Hanif's letters still in her bag. At the train station she'd walked back and forth past the rubbish bin outside the ladies' waiting room. Finally, at home that afternoon, when a drowsy silence pervaded the house, she returned the letters to their original hiding place in the armoire.

Now here was Hanif at the cricket stadium, standing a few feet from her. 'I've kept your letters,' she wanted to tell him, 'I couldn't just throw them away.'

Instead, she said nothing; she couldn't even meet his eye.

'Well . . . quite a match,' Iqbalji said.

Nobody said anything.

'We should be going,' Iqbalji said, turning to Hanif.

Hanif had the urge to run, to get away from the clubhouse as quickly as possible; but he couldn't move.

Nalin raised his hand in a wave.

'Goodbye,' Saroj said. 'We're waiting for Rohini's . . .' she motioned with her hand at the gents' room.

Hanif looked in the direction. The man . . . Rohini's . . . O, *Allah-ki-Madad*, she had come to the cricket match with *him*! His eyes skipped between the gents' sign and Rohini. At any moment the door would open and *he* would walk out. Hanif went over the other men he'd seen inside. There were three men in the sitting room and he couldn't have been any of them, they were much too old. And definitely not the fellow talking on the telephone or the man coughing loudly – they were both British. That left the tall man with the expensive shoes. Hanif tried to recall the man's face, but couldn't, not fully; however, he remembered the man was wearing glasses. Hanif imagined the idiot walking out and smiling at Rohini, and she smiling back, and he and Rohini talking about things with a familiarity that Hanif knew once existed between Rohini and himself. The blood began thumping loudly in his ears. The idiot had sat next to Rohini during the cricket match, and he must have leaned over, brushing her shoulder while explaining the details of the game.

'Let's go,' Iqbalji said, taking Hanif's elbow. 'The match is not over yet.'

As they walked down the corridor to their seats Hanif could feel Rohini's gentle eyes on his back. He heard the gents' door open, but he didn't turn around.

The drizzle turned into a slow steady rain. There was a chance play would be called off on account of rain and India could escape with a draw. The umpire looked at his watch and then gestured with both hands for the players to continue. Wally Hamming, the English captain, hit a six on the first ball. The numbers on the scoreboard slowly changed.

'I think we've been beaten,' Iqbalji said, shaking his head and stabbing the point of his umbrella on the ground.

Chapter 17

Rohini spotted Pervez – his hair overgrown, face unshaven, eyes bloodshot – buying a newspaper from the kiosk at Marine Lines station. At least his clothes were clean and ironed. 'Everything's okay. Really,' he said when she asked how he was. She looked at him for a long moment – a severe, direct gaze – and he felt compelled to explain himself to her. He folded the newspaper, tucked it under his arm. 'Come on, we'll be late for college. I'll tell you on the way.'

Pervez said he had joined the Indian People's Theater and become fast friends with the organization's leaders who were staunch supporters of the Communist Party of India. 'It all happened quickly,' he said, 'Before I knew it, there I was at a fundraising event talking with the big leaders of the CPI, and everything just fell into place.'

The CPI was planning a major demonstration. 'We can't estimate the size, but we've decided that it will be most effective if there are simultaneous demonstrations in several parts of the city.' They walked past the sari shops, and Kayani's bakery. 'There is some possibility of violence,' Pervez said, lowering his voice. 'So we're buying steel pipes, also smoke bombs and guns.'

'Guns!' Rohini said, fighting the urge to shout it out. 'Have you gone mad or what?'

'Say what you want, but it's a good cause,' Pervez said.

'You might get killed! Others might get killed.' Rohini shook her head. 'What about America? I thought you were going abroad for studies,' she said, and added, though she wasn't sure why, 'My brother's going to America.'

'America can wait. There are more important things going on here. Don't you see?'

'No. I don't see,' Rohini said, glaring at him. 'What's in your shirt pocket? You've started smoking . . .'

'I know what I'm doing,' he said. 'Remember, not a word to anyone.'

'About your cigarettes?'

'No,' he said gruffly, patting his shirt pocket. 'About the CPI.'

'It's dangerous . . .'

Pervez said, 'I kept your secret, didn't I?'

Her throat tightened. 'But this . . .'

'Promise me?' he said.

She nodded and they continued in silence the rest of the way to college.

Chapter 18

Saroj hummed as she approached the armoire in the bedroom. It was a massive piece of furniture with four doors, made of Burmese teak and polished to a dark sheen. The doors, carved with an intricate floral pattern, had swirled brass handles and a full-length bevelled mirror covered the middle section.

Most of the shelves contained untidy heaps of her sister's things. Saroj and her two young children were visiting from Dantali for a few weeks and on a couple of shelves her own saris were systematically stacked in two piles – 'going out' and 'staying in' – and then further sorted by colour. Saroj glanced at the desk. If she were in college she would keep her papers and books in better order. She would tidy up the armoire, and then take on the desk.

Saroj tucked the end of her sari more firmly at her waist. Despite the herbal tonics she took every day, she seemed to tire easily. After sorting the armoire and desk, she would take a nap, and then ask for her afternoon tea by the front verandah. Motilal and Harshaba were in Ahmedabad for several days and the house seemed to have taken on an easier rhythm.

She spread an old white bedsheet on the floor and began

removing the saris, the pleasing smell of silk and cotton, washing soap and starch drifting out. Some of the petticoats were frayed, the hem separating from the lace, and she put these in a separate pile for the tailor to mend.

On the lowest shelf, tucked behind Rohini's 'special' saris, she found a small silk-wrapped bundle. And another, half-covered by a Kashmiri shawl. And here, another one. They were all carefully knotted. Money? Unlikely. But it felt like paper.

She rummaged to make sure she hadn't missed any and carried them to the bed, on which she sat cross-legged, and untied the knots. Letters. To Rohini. From Hanif. Hanif? A Muslim name. The other bundles were also letters, again addressed to Rohini and written by the same Hanif. The handwriting was clear and the words composed by a well-educated mind; the paper was white and lined, from a cheap writing pad.

Saroj began reading. Her eyes narrowed in concentration. After a few minutes she stood up and locked the bedroom door. A small blue vein at her temple began to twitch. She glanced at the open windows. A humid, cloudy afternoon stretched outside. She closed the windows before returning to the letters strewn on the floor.

She found a few chits, written in a hand less careful than the letters. *Metro, 3:30 on Saturday*, on a folded piece of paper. *Wait near Bandra bus depot.* That was written on the back of a café receipt. *Cafe Royal on Sunday* was scribbled on a page torn from an exercise book. A sheet of blue paper, excessively creased from being folded and unfolded many times, turned out to be a cyclostyled announcement for a poetry reading. A flimsy brown envelope contained used tickets from cinema houses. Saroj checked the dates on the letters and re-read some of the pages. Her eyes paused at one of the poems:

Like water in the desert
You are the expression of my thoughts;
In every breath of my being, it is you, only you.
I dream of you each night, and wake to a world more beautiful than yesterday.
The hope of seeing you fills my mind with unimaginable
    bliss;
Without you, nothing.

The fervour of the words, the earnestness, the spontaneity, the underlying passion that filled these letters . . . Saroj had never dared imagine such romance in her life. In her nights with her husband, there was nothing exciting, intense, or exotic, only a sense of duty that propelled her to give herself to him. She rifled through the letters, scanning the lower portion of each page for more poems.

Those stubborn tides of longing,
The joy of our meetings,
The melancholy tears of farewell.

On another page:

Against the soft hush of your silences,
And the quiet dance of flowers, so pure, so delicate,
Your scattered smiles speak—
Be still, be still my trembling heart.

She had read enough to understand what was going on, but she couldn't help herself. She kept reading, consuming each line with fiery curiosity.

Saroj finished the last of the letters, looked for a while towards the window, letting the thrill of her illicit discovery subside, then crossed to the mirror. She traced her fingers over the contours of her nose, her chin, and the mole at her mouth. Her centre-parted hair, pinned in a bun, was greying at the temples. She stared at herself. She had given up the carefree years of her youth to take on the burdens of marriage. She had done what was expected of her and held fast with vigour. There should have been reward in that, but no – life had cheated her of enchantment. She had extracted comfort from the routine of daily life, but what she had wanted was a different contentment. Turning her head, she studied her profile in the mirror. She pulled the sari off her shoulders and regarded her breasts, drooping after two children.

Why had *she* been denied the romance proffered in those letters? Why had *she* been barred from the sweetness that laced those lines of poetry? She reached both hands to her hairpins, and watched in the mirror as the bun unravelled; thinning hair hung limp to her shoulders.

If this man had written such letters, surely Rohini had written similar letters to him. What amorous words had Rohini penned? The magnitude of the situation loomed before her like a mountain becoming visible through dissipating mist.

Hanif . . . that was the name of the man they'd run into at the cricket club. After the match Rohini, Jagmohan, Nalin and Saroj had gone to the Grand Hotel for tea – how pale and quiet Rohini had been, sitting upright on the sofa next to Jagmohan, tense and ready to flee. She hadn't eaten a thing.

Saroj glanced at the clock and started putting her hair up.

Rohini wouldn't be home for at least another three hours. Crouching on her knees, she gathered the letters and, placing them diagonally on the square handkerchiefs, retied the bundles.

ಸಃ

As the train snaked through millet fields and cow pastures and over the Narmada Bridge, Saroj found it difficult to sleep. Motilal and Harshaba would be horrified at the news; she had no idea how they would deal with Rohini, and this worried her. She could pretend she'd never seen those letters or she could have burned them and let the matter quietly fall away. But no. She tossed in the lower berth as the train hurtled towards Ahmedabad.

Chimanji Baug was a stately mansion on ten acres at the edge of the Sabarmati, the banks of which were dotted with neem and jackfruit trees, as well as tall, wispy reeds that sprouted flowers from time to time. Water buffalos lazed in the river, their black forms submerged with only the round of their backs, horns, and snouts visible over the surface. Most of the year the house was empty and it had an air of benign neglect. Now, because of the upcoming wedding, the house was a hive of activity – Motilal was having it repainted and refurbished because Harshaba wanted to host a dinner party for a hundred guests the week before the wedding. The large cracks in the marble steps leading from the porch to the front door were being repaired and all the brass work polished.

In the main drawing room Saroj sat next to Harshaba on

the sofa, Motilal in a chair across from them. Bamboo scaffolding leaned against the walls and yards of old fabric covered the furniture. Stuttering and pausing, Saroj told them of her discovery. Motilal's face darkened. He leaned back in the chair, his mouth slightly open, and looked upwards, as though expecting divine guidance. '*Mussalman!* Mussalman!' Harshaba said, her breath short and quick, and the room filled with the sounds of her sobbing.

Motilal asked, 'Are you sure about all this? Absolutely sure?'

'Yes,' Saroj said.

'We must have done some horrible thing in our past lives,' Harshaba said, looking unhappily at Motilal. She dabbed her eyes with the edge of her sari. 'A Muslim, why a Muslim?'

'Christian or Parsi or Sikh would have been okay?' Motilal said, trying to hide his rising fury behind sarcasm. 'What about an *Angrez?*' He spat the word.

'Why are you being irrational at a time like this? Oh, what a thing to happen,' Harshaba moaned. Then another panic set in. 'What about Jagmohan? What do we say to his parents?' Harshaba resumed sobbing, more loudly, and she could be heard around the house.

'What do we say to the world?' Motilal said, putting his head in his hands. 'Where did she meet this Muslim?' he said, staring at the floor.

'At college . . . I think,' Saroj replied.

'College!' Harshaba spat the word. 'See, I told you from the beginning. Girls should not go to college. What was the need? College is not meant for Hindu girls. What is wrong with reading the Ramayana and Mahabharata? Our books teach everything. I told you not to allow this,' she said to Motilal. Then, turning to Saroj with blazing eyes and pointing an index finger at her face, Harshaba shouted, 'This is your fault!'

'My fault? How?'

'Yes, your fault. A Muslim. My daughter and a Muslim!'

'I don't understand. My fault?' Saroj looked at Harshaba, then at Motilal.

Harshaba's face was on fire. 'Yes, your fault, Saroj. You're the one who insisted that Rohini go to college. I remember. We should never have listened to you.'

'You can be angry with me if you wish,' Saroj said in a trembling voice, 'but think of Rohini.'

'No college. Rohini cannot go to college anymore,' Harshaba said, throwing the words out like arrows, and Motilal nodded in agreement.

'But . . .'

Harshaba's curses drowned her out and as she began a diatribe on sinful, meat-eating Muslims, Motilal slumped in his chair, a deep sadness spreading over his face.

Saroj said, 'Please, she must finish college and get her degree.'

Harshaba glared at Saroj. 'No more college. Enough!' Harshaba stomped one foot on the floor in exclamation.

Motilal, regaining his composure, said, 'We'd better inform the Shahs. Should we go to their house now?'

Saroj stared at the ground. Soon everyone in Ahmedabad would know, and then word would spread to Bombay. Pernicious tongues would gossip about a broken engagement. An affair with a Muslim.

Harshaba arose from the sofa and paced in front of Saroj

and Motilal. 'There's no need to tell the Shahs anything,' she said. 'Rohini will marry Jagmohan. No one must know about Rohini and the Muslim. We'll return to Bombay immediately. The wedding preparations must continue. Our honour is at stake.'

Motilal's face turned pale and his jaw twitched. He looked alternately at Harshaba and Saroj.

'It's the only way,' Harshaba said. 'Otherwise, she will never be able to marry. Don't you see?'

'But, wait,' Saroj said. 'If Rohini doesn't finish college, the Shahs will . . .' Her voice trailed off and she heard Harshaba's raspy breathing. 'Jagmohan will ask . . .' Saroj said timidly. 'Jagmohan will ask about her degree.'

Motilal shifted in his chair, put his head in his hands again. Saroj looked away to avoid meeting her mother's wrathful face. She had gone too far, but it was the only way to help Rohini. 'Oh,' Harshaba said. 'In that case . . . when does she finish?'

Chapter 19

Motilal had faced humiliation once before, when he first moved from Ahmedabad to Bombay. It was almost twenty years ago, but sometimes the memory flashed into his mind unbidden and it felt like it had only just happened. Dressed in a white dhoti and kurta, Motilal was on Chowpatty beach watching flocks of seagulls swooping around the shore. He had brought his wife and children to the beach for the first time the day before – it was Sunday and they had all stood in a semi-circle watching the *bunder-walla* directing his acrobatic monkeys, and then walked a little way down the beach to where the snake charmers squatted with their cobra baskets. The children had ridden the rickety merry-go-round while Motilal and Harshaba had watched them from under an awning. He'd bought peanuts for the children because the ice-candy was too expensive, but it had been a happy evening, and as they walked home to their cramped flat on Sandhurst Road, he was glad they had moved to Bombay.

After strolling for a while, Motilal found a bench on the edge of the beach. The sun had made its exit, leaving behind a gently lit sky. A breeze from the Arabian Sea moved the pleats of his dhoti between his ankles. He leaned back on the bench. He could hear the waves and seagulls, and behind him the low, familiar din of the city when he sensed someone approaching. Two men were moving purposefully towards him – a British naval officer, carrying his hat by its visor, face pink and blotchy from the Bombay sun, and a slightly built Indian, barefoot, in baggy short pants and an oversized shirt. The officer stopped in front of Motilal and in one swift official motion put his hat on his head and gestured with his index finger for Motilal to stand.

Motilal hadn't given much thought to the whole business of British rule in India. It was all he had ever known and his family had made ends meet regardless. He stood up slowly. His feet were half removed from his chappals, so he shuffled to get them on properly. He put both palms on his chest and tried to smooth out his kurta. Images of the 1919 Amritsar massacre where General Dyer ordered his troops to fire on hundreds of unarmed Indians flashed through his mind as he stared at the buttons of the officer's uniform.

'What's your name, chap?'

The gruffness of the officer's tone frightened him, but he tried to stay calm and remain cooperative. The small Indian stood at attention behind the officer, his dark eyes looking straight ahead, and he translated in Hindi: '*Aap ka naam bataiyeh?*'

'Motilal. Uh, uh . . . Chimanji,' Motilal whispered, his eyes bouncing between the officer's face and the Indian's.

'Mistah Chimanji,' the officer said. 'It is after sunset and you have no right to be here. That is the *law*,' the last word shouted in Motilal's face, making him step backwards. Spray from the officer's mouth landed on Motilal's face, and he reached up to wipe it off, immediately regretting the movement.

'*Shaam ho chuki heh. Aap yahan nehin reh sakte,*' the assistant translated in Hindi.

'*Meh su goono karyo che?*' Motilal asked quietly in Gujurati. 'What have I done wrong?'

'Tell him to clear the beach immediately!' the officer commanded, which the assistant promptly translated, following on with the officer's next utterance, 'We don't need any trouble. Understand.' Under his breath he hissed, 'Bloody Indians.' The assistant did not translate this, but Motilal understood.

Motilal's timidity gave way to boldness and there followed a series of increasingly caustic exchanges. The assistant tried his best to keep up with the translations. Motilal insisted that he had every right to be on the beach, even after sunset, because the beach belonged to everyone. Then, surprised and empowered by his own effrontery, Motilal stamped his foot in the sand and said this was India, and since he was Indian he had even more of a right to be on that beach or, for that matter, anywhere on Indian soil that he pleased. The officer, his voice getting louder, more belligerent, catching only fragments of what his assistant translated, kept firing general insults about Indians at Motilal who reiterated his stance, his voice trembling but resolute. The assistant didn't know where to look, or what to translate.

Motilal was marched to a nearby police station, where he was issued a citation that required him to appear in court and pay two fines – one for sitting on the beach after sunset, and the other for talking improperly to a British officer.

In his final steps off the beach, with the officer gripping his arm, almost tearing his shoulder out, and the assistant shuffling behind them, Motilal decided to build a house on the beach. He would gaze at the sunset whenever he pleased.

The idea of the house became his own private struggle against the British, and it consumed him to the point where he would lay awake for hours at night envisioning his house on the beach, building in his mind imaginary rooms, verandahs, porticos, and prayer halls, moving walls each night to accommodate this or that. The house kept growing. His imagination, and his frustration with the British, knew no bounds.

Motilal's silk business reaped unprecedented profit – the gods and goddesses were on his side, he believed – and he bought a plot of land at Versova, about fifteen miles north of the city. When construction on the house began, Motilal stood alongside the *majdurs*, encouraging them as they dug and shovelled and hammered. At midday he sat on a chair, perched on a pile of rubble, put up an umbrella against the sun, and ate the lunch that Harshaba had packed in three round containers of a tiffin box, the *lassi* in an old glass rose-syrup bottle. At dusk, dusty with construction debris, he would strut around surveying the progress of the day. When the monsoon blew, from June through August, the waves leaped high above the compound wall; but even as the water crashed around him and the salty foam itched his skin, Motilal stood alongside the majdurs and insisted they keep working.

By the end of the third monsoon, construction was complete. The house, the glorious manifestation of Motilal's humiliation, was stately and grand. It's a palace by the sea, someone said, so Motilal named it *Sagar Mahal*.

Chapter 20

While getting ready for college Rohini was surprised to hear her mother's voice shouting for the servants to help with the luggage. Her parents weren't supposed to return from Ahmedabad for another ten days. Her sisters, Sumitra and Amrita were still asleep, but she doubted they would be allowed to remain so for long.

There was a tentative knock and Saroj stood in the doorway, a tired figure in a crumpled beige sari.

'Saroj, you're back from Ahmedabad – so soon? I'm just leaving for college. Tutorials today. I'll be home by tea time.'

Her sister, smiling lightly, did not move from the doorway, blocking her way. 'The Muslim,' Saroj said. 'They know about the Muslim.'

'What?'

'The man from your college . . . Hanif?'

Rohini's face blanched, her chin dropped. She backed away from her sister and leaned against the sofa. How had they found out? Why was this happening now?

'I found his letters.'

Rohini's eyes darted to the armoire.

Saroj's gaze followed. 'Yes. In there.'

'But . . . you don't understand,' Rohini whispered. 'Th-those letters. They mean nothing. Really. Nothing.'

'How can you say that? I read them myself!'

Rohini felt unsteady and sat on her rumpled bed. She tried to work out what Saroj may have read; perhaps there was an innocent explanation for what they said. Rohini had practically memorized the letters, yet now she couldn't recall a single sentence.

'They want you to finish exams,' Saroj said.

'You . . . you told them? Why? Why would you do that?'

'I insisted that you finish your college degree,' Saroj said. 'You are to come straight home. Every day.'

Rohini felt dizzy.

'Go now,' Saroj said, 'before they finish their baths and their pujas. Just go. They'll talk to you in the evening. Be prepared.'

'So that's why you rushed off to Ahmedabad?'

'Just go.'

'I see . . . You were snooping among my things, found my private correspondence, read the letters, and then decided the only course of action was for you to go immediately to Ahmedabad to tell them.' Rohini glared at Saroj, then stood up slowly. A tear leaked out and trickled down her cheek. 'Why?'

'Why?'

'Why did you tell them?' Rohini's voice shook.

'Look, it doesn't matter. Be sensible . . .'

'Sensible? You're telling me to be sensible? *You* went running to Ahmedabad. Why weren't *you* sensible? *Why did you tell them?*'

Saroj glared at Rohini, 'Don't talk to me like that. I don't believe . . .'

'You betrayed me!' Rohini said, her voice quivering. 'You could have come to me first. You could have waited, given me a chance to explain. Instead, you took matters into your own hands. Why are you always in Bombay? Why don't you stay in Dantali where you belong! I'm tired of you interfering in my life.' She'd never talked to her sister in this tone. 'Why did you look through my clothes? You had no business going through my things! What's wrong with you? You didn't feel an ounce of shame?' A wall as high as the Red Fort was rising between them. 'I know what it is. You hate living in Dantali, you hate being married to your ugly husband, and you hate your . . . your *dull* life. You wish *you* could have gone to college, and you wish *you* could have married someone like Hanif . . .'

Twap. The slap landed squarely and horribly on Rohini's cheek and, as she flinched from the impact, reflexively raising her hands to shield her face, the second slap landed lower, across her mouth.

'Get out!' Saroj yelled. She reached for Rohini's book bag and flung it across the room. The bag clattered into the neatly arranged bottles on the dressing table. 'You should go live in a gutter somewhere. I have no sympathy for you. I can't believe you're my sister!' She thrust her hand in the air, as though in victory: 'You *cannot* have your Muslim. You cannot disgrace this family. You *will* marry Jagmohan.'

Rohini wanted to dig her fingers into Saroj's face, into her eyes, claw at the malice that had dripped from those last words. She bent to the floor to retrieve the contents of her bag, tears now streaming down her raw cheek, which glistened with fury and defeat.

ನ್ನ

Without stopping for morning tea, without greeting her parents, and without returning the chowkidar's *salaam* at the gate, Rohini hurried to college. On the way to the bus stand, she didn't notice Ramchander opening the shutters at Ramchander's Provisions, or his wife sweeping the ground in front of the shop. The clanging bells at the small temple near the bus stand seemed to match her thudding heart. On the bus to the station, and then for the entire train ride to college, a new panic infused her mind – Saroj had gone to Ahmedabad and now everyone there knew. Jag knew. Everybody would know. The whole world would know.

She sat through the tutorials in a daze. She wrote some lines in her notebook: 'The most realistic of Shakespeare's love comedies. Realistic, despite the basic improbability. Written during the reign of Elizabeth. Sustained, mimetic realism furthered by complex, romantically stylized dialogue.' She heard the professor compare the portrayal of love in *Much Ado About Nothing* to *Romeo and Juliet* and *Twelfth Night*, but she couldn't grasp his analysis. She tried to imagine what her parents were going to say that evening. After college, she walked to the station, her head down.

On the train some students were talking about Subhas Chandra Bose: 'He wanted to fight the British with an army, but he didn't have Gandhi's support.' 'He had the support of the Soviet Union, Nazi Germany, and Japan! Wasn't that enough?' She tried to focus on the conversation. 'The British army in India was comprised of Indian soldiers – shouldn't they have fought to free India instead of fighting to keep the Raj?' 'Whole units went over to the Japs in Malaya.' 'And after the fall of Singapore.' The train stopped several times and people flowed in and out. From the bridge over Mahim creek she saw the old factories, and the large sewer pipes that ran above ground, dumping their foul-smelling liquid contents straight into the creek. Along the pipes, she noticed hutment colonies, where the roofs were thatched with palm leaves and sheets of discarded plastic. She felt a sudden pang of sympathy for these thousands who had come from drought-ridden parts of India to find work in the city.

When she arrived home, the house was strangely silent. None of the usual bustle at this hour between the kitchen and the divankhana, tea being readied on the verandah, servants sweeping and dusting, gardeners weeding and trimming. Even the twittering birds seemed to be holding their breath.

Rohini went directly to her room. For a long time she sat in the armchair by the window looking out at the sea – the water, abundant and ancient, offered temporary solace. Finally, she rang for the ayah, who barged in, eyes wide with alarm. 'They've gone,' the ayah said. 'They have all gone to hospital. Motilalji. Suddenly he collapsed. They have taken him to hospital.'

Chapter 21

On the bench outside Motilal's room at the hospital, Harshaba's eyes were swollen from weeping. 'If he goes, how will I handle everything?' she asked no one in particular. Saroj, Sumitra, Amrita, Mahesh, Shrikant and Prema were waiting with her to hear the doctor's diagnosis. Saroj tried to focus Harshaba's mind on the facts of the matter. 'How did this happen? He's always been in such good health . . .'

Motilal had finished his bath and, with a dhoti around his waist and a towel around his shoulders, was on his way to the dressing room when he felt dizzy. Harshaba heard the crash of a pot and found Motilal on the floor, amid shards of clay and a pool of spreading water. Trying to steady himself he'd reached for the stand that held an earthen water pot and knocked it over. She yelled for help and then rushed to summon the doctor. Dr Kapoor was there within minutes, wielding a stethoscope and smelling salts. Everyone was relieved when Motilal opened his eyes, but Harshaba started sobbing when Dr Kapoor said Motilal should be admitted to hospital for some tests.

ೱೱ

Rohini entered Motilal's hospital room taking slow, small steps. She half-hoped he was asleep and she could slip out again unnoticed. On the ledge behind the sink were his toiletries – shaving items, a comb, and a red plastic soapbox – and his brown suitcase lay next to the bed on a chair. Saroj must have unpacked his clothes into the drawers.

'You've come,' Motilal said dully. He wore a white kurta, the outline of his undershirt visible through the thin fabric. He was reclining in the bed on two pillows. The white sheet and grey blanket that covered him from the waist down were tucked tightly under the mattress.

'Yes,' she said, standing at the foot of the bed. She could see herself in a mirror above the drawers – the white pattern of her sari matched her pearl necklace. She reached a hand to adjust the spray of white jasmines she'd pinned in her hair that morning. Outside the room she had tried to sit on the bench with her mother, but Harshaba had glared and turned away. Rohini wondered if her father, too, would refuse to talk to her.

'You're studying for exams?' he asked.

'Yes,' Rohini said, her eyes cast to the tiled white floor.

'Uh . . . what about?' Motilal looked towards a green flask on the side table.

'Do you want something to drink?' she said, stepping towards the side table.

He gestured 'no' with his hand. Her father had never punished her before, and she braced herself now for his severe tone.

'Have you seen the new currency?' he said. 'No more Queen on the notes.'

Rohini looked up at him and smiled slightly.

She was reminded of a day, almost five years ago, when thousands of bright yellow leaflets were scattered over the city exhorting people to defy the British Raj: *Videshi vastuon ka bahishkar* – 'Boycott foreign-made goods.' At home, over the shrieks of her younger sisters, she had poured the entire contents of a crystal bottle of English Lavender *eau de cologne* into the sink. Even earlier, in 1930, Gandhi had led a two-hundred-mile march to the sea to protest the Salt Tax, implored Indian civil servants to resign from the British government, and advocated a boycott on imported British cloth in favour of homespun cotton. All these actions had invited brutal reprisals and, when British barbarism elicited worldwide attention, the resulting concessions had always been more symbolic than concrete. It had been a long, difficult road to Independence. She thought now about the new currency that depicted lions on a pillar. 'Yes, I've seen the ten-rupee note,' she said. 'Ashoka pillar, sandstone, fifth century,' she added, as though she were being tested.

'What is everyone at college saying about . . . Partition?' Motilal asked.

'Everyone at college thinks Congress is compromising . . .'

Motilal interjected, 'But this is what the Muslims want, no?' He crumpled the edge of the sheet in his fist and looked away. 'How is Pervez?' he asked. 'Do you see him at college? I meet his father from time to time. I decided that Mahesh should go to America because Pervez . . .'

'I don't think Pervez is going to America.' She wondered what new communist adventure Pervez was involved in. Her eyes went to the window, which was filled with a view of the iridescent orange flowers on the gulmohar tree outside.

'Pervez's father is having new suits stitched for him at Davysons.'

'Oh, I see,' Rohini said. The overhead fan moved the air in the room with a rhythmical squeaking. A sparrow chirped excitedly as it flitted about in the gulmohar, leaping from branch to branch, then flying away.

'I've never been to America,' he said, and Rohini was surprised at his wistful tone. There were voices of other visitors outside the door. A nurse carrying a tray came bustling in. 'Your exams are soon?' he said.

'Yes,' Rohini said. 'I'll go now.'

ಬಿ

Saroj approached Harshaba while she was taking her morning tea on the verandah outside the kitchen at Sagar Mahal. From here there was a view of the full expanse of the front gardens – the almond trees, the bamboos, the Roman fountain, and the freshwater well in the corner. A poppy-embroidered tablecloth covered the table before them; the breeze lifted the edges of the cloth and as Saroj bent forward to hold it down, she asked her mother, 'Have you spoken to Rohini about . . .?'

'Have I had time? The last three days have been spent at hospital with your father.' Harshaba leaned into the bench, adjusting the cushion behind her. Her face looked weary. Dark crescents edged her otherwise vigilant eyes. Dr Kapoor had told her that Motilal's heart condition had to be monitored in hospital. But he was out of danger and would recover with no lasting ill effects.

'I was planning to leave for Dantali tomorrow,' Saroj said. 'I can stay if you need me.'

'A woman's place is with her husband,' Harshaba said in a measured tone. 'How many times do I have to tell you that?'

ಬಃ

Vincent, the driver, had just finished washing the Vauxhall when Harshaba sent for him. He draped the chamois on the dark green hood of the car, dried his hands on his frayed undershirt, and hurried towards the main portico. He had ironed his driver's uniform that morning – white long pants, white jacket with shiny buttons. He knew he looked smart in it, especially with the white hat and black shoes that completed the uniform.

Vincent looked up at the sky as he walked towards the house. Why did he bother washing the car during the rainy season? It would be splattered with mud as soon as he pulled out of the gates.

Harshaba handed him a list.

Vincent glanced at it quizzically, mentally going over the sundry items. He didn't mind doing the shopping, but he didn't like how Harshaba hassled him about not bargaining with the shops for a lower price. 'Not today,' he said.

'Why not?' Harshaba crossed her arms over her chest.

'Sahib is in hospital,' Vincent answered in a straightforward tone. 'I can't drive to the city today.' He folded the list and handed it back to Harshaba.

Chapter 22

At Café Royal, Rohini tried to pay attention to what Pervez was saying. 'My father wants me to go to America, but I could be a leader here. I could serve the country . . .' But her mind kept drifting. Nothing had changed. The restaurant smelled as it always did, of oil and sugar and milk. Pervez talked of grand plans, as he always did. By now, the whole world knew of her romance with Hanif. She had admired Saroj, respected her serene demeanor, the quiet order and logic with which she approached each task. Saroj had routinely spoken up for her, and now it occurred to Rohini that it had all been an act, a charade, a build-up for this momentous betrayal. Pressing a palm to her cheek she felt the rage of Saroj's fingers anew. She was dreading the conversation with her parents, of explaining the unfortunate desires of her heart. She had tried to conjure up scenarios from her favourite novels that might impart some wisdom, but nothing came to mind. Even the fictional world had deserted her. She couldn't bear the thought of Jag . . . of marrying him and both of them living with the knowledge that she'd wanted to marry another. She recalled the time in the bazaar during the kite festival in Ahmedabad when she had tried to tell him the truth.

'Saroj found his letters,' she said to Pervez, cutting him off, and told him everything in a shaky voice. She reached in her bag, 'Here, I can't bring myself to throw them away. Please return them to him.'

Pervez eyed the silken bundles and backed away from the table. 'You should give them to him yourself. I'll ask him to meet you at Metro Cinema tomorrow. Four o'clock. Okay?'

After several moments of hesitation, she nodded her head.

'Good,' Pervez said. He looked at her sorrowful face and thought he saw there a flicker of excitement.

ಬಿ

'What if she comes there with her father?' Hanif asked Pervez, but didn't expect an answer. 'I refuse, I will not go. I will not go anywhere *near* Metro Cinema tomorrow.'

'But I've already told her. She'll be waiting.'

'Let her wait. I am not going!'

ಬಿ

But he was there, early, outside Metro. The city was trapped in a downpour and traffic was forced to a crawling-honking-halting pace. Gutters overflowed into the road, and black umbrellas, broken and twisted, erratically rode the flow. A new picture was playing at Metro and Hanif stood under the marquee reading the credits on the multicoloured poster. Always a stellar cast – Nargis Dutt, Dilip Kumar, Raj Kapoor. Hanif continued down the list, reading the names of producers, directors, sound technicians, editors, and choreographers. A few pedestrians hurried along the footpath around him. He didn't regret the letters he'd written, but felt embarrassed that someone else had read the intimate lines. Inside the box office a man whistled cheerfully over his paperwork. Hanif could see the plush space of the lobby through the smudged glass doors of the cinema house – the chandeliers, the sofas and tables, and the concession stands beyond.

Rohini came directly from college, the hem of her sari soaked from the rain. It was the first day of exams, but it hardly mattered anymore. She was going through the hours without interest, without hope. Yet the anxiety now. And the joyous quickening of her heart. She'd brought his letters; should she just hand them over and leave?

Hanif was standing, one hand in his pant pocket, the other holding a dripping umbrella. The sleeves of his white shirt were un-cuffed and rolled just above the wrists. She thought he smiled when he saw her.

They stood silently for a few moments under the awning while the rain, an incessant deluge, fell around them. A man pushing a cart, his load covered and tied in plastic, trundled along the footpath. She stepped out of the way and Hanif lifted his hand to shield her from the cart. It was a slight gesture, hardly noticeable, but something inside her leapt with excitement.

'Let's go inside,' Hanif pointed towards the glass doors.

Rohini nodded as she closed her umbrella.

The attendant at the box office shouted as he saw them. Hanif looked at him impatiently, went to purchase tickets; the attendant took the money, shoved the tickets at Hanif, and urged them to hurry because the picture had already begun.

'Pervez told me what happened,' Hanif said. 'Here, let's sit.'

Except for a lanky security guard wandering around, the lobby was empty. In the concession area two uniformed attendants arranged bottles of drinks and snacks wrapped in wax paper. Beyond the concession area the big black doors that opened onto the lower seats of the theater were closed; the wide marble staircase that led to the mezzanine and balcony seating stood silent and grand.

'Something to eat? Drink?' Hanif asked.

She shook her head, sitting stiffly in the sofa.

'So, how are you?' Hanif sat opposite her. He crossed his ankles, and moved one arm to the armrest. He noticed her eyes, watery and flecked with redness. She looked different; the brightness and exuberance had gone from her face.

'I'm okay,' she said with a weak smile. 'And you? You won the music competition.' Her eyes rested on his neck, and she watched the muscles move as he swallowed and cleared his throat. She'd forgotten that little gesture of his – the deep, punctuating sound that he sometimes made.

'Yes,' he replied. He had chosen as his final song the one about the bumblebee. *Raatein thi chandani joban pe thi bahaar . . .*

'My congratulations. I should have . . .' She felt self-conscious. She thought about the concert hall and crowds of people and what if felt like to be applauded. She gave him a sidelong look. Her shameful hope was that Hanif would never marry. She wanted him to be a successful musician, but . . . it had never occurred to her until then to be jealous.

Hanif looked away. 'They gave me a one year recording contract with HMV.'

She smiled brightly and nodded.

'And you?' he asked. 'You'll be living in Ahmedabad?'

'Yes,' she said, eyes to the floor.

The big doors that led to the theater opened and a woman and child emerged from the dark space. The sounds of actors shouting, and loud, suspenseful music drifted into the lobby. The door closed and it was quiet again. The woman and child walked towards the concession stand.

'Have you seen it?' Hanif pointed towards the door, reminded of happier times when they'd sat together inside the theater. He thought about her small, smooth hand resting in his. The first time he put his arm around her shoulder – in the darkness he'd felt her entire body stiffen, then she'd leaned her head on his shoulder and he'd stared at the screen feeling certain he understood the meaning of bliss. He fished for the tickets in his shirt pocket but knew there was no chance of them seeing the film.

'No,' she said, 'I haven't seen any pictures since . . .'

The rain outside had not abated and the road signs and billboards were flapping in the wind.

The woman and child walked back from the concession stand. The child, contemplating the snack he was given, trailed a few steps behind. The woman held the door open for him, and again, the sounds of the film escaped into the lobby. This time it was a song sequence with a frolicking, staccato rhythm, a lead female voice, and a chorus of other voices. The door closed behind them, and stillness returned to the lobby.

Rohini looked at Hanif. 'We should get married,' she said, surprised at her own words, how normal and simple and logical she sounded.

Hanif looked incredulous.

'You and I should get married,' she said, her voice strong and urgent. There in the lobby of Metro Cinema, between the fantasy world of the pictures and the reality of existence in the city, between the songs on the luminous screen and the driving rain outside, everything was clear to her.

'But . . . but you're engaged. What about your . . .'

Rohini turned away, anxious that she had spoken rashly thoughts that should have stayed inside her head. 'We won't tell anyone,' she said, talking quickly, looking directly into his eyes.

'You mean . . .? What exactly?' Hanif's chin dropped. 'At a mosque?' He ran a shaky hand through his coal-black hair.

She blinked nervously. She'd never set foot inside a mosque. 'Yes,' she said. 'That way no one will know. My parents will not approve, but it doesn't matter.'

Hanif could only stare at her. She was engaged to another man, a rich Hindu, and now she was willing to walk away from her life and marry him. His mind raced, his breathing short and quick. One of his legs began twitching. He tried to imagine her at the mosque on Fridays, praying with the other women behind the latticed partition, but all he saw was her face in front of him now, her eyes fixed on his.

'All right,' he whispered. 'Let's get married.' A broad grin broke across his face.

They sat there, Rohini on the sofa and Hanif in the armchair, looking at each other, ensconced in their secret, giddy in their emotion. The security guard sauntered past, oblivious to the drama that had just unfolded, and muttered something about money and tickets and missing a good picture.

'We should do it quickly,' she said. 'As soon as possible. Before anything happens. Before anyone finds out.' Her eyes darted about the lobby.

He leaned forward and took both her hands in his. 'Are you absolutely sure?'

'Oh, yes,' she replied, her hands delighting at his touch. 'Exams finish on Thursday, on the fourteenth . . .'

'Right, so after your exams finish on the fourteenth, come straight to Churchgate. I'll meet you near the ticket counter. Under the clock.' His thoughts rolled over the details. It was Monday. They would be married in three days!

'Okay,' she said, a smile spreading over her face.

'You'll be there? Promise?' he asked.

'God promise,' she said.

Hanif wondered for a flicker of a second whose God, but he didn't ask.

She added, 'You know the next day, on the fifteenth . . .?'

'Yes, I know. Independence Day. The British are leaving.' He felt a renewed excitement. 'The bumblebee,' he said.

'What?'

'The song at the competition was about a bumblebee.'

She laughed. 'Really? I haven't heard that song. You'll sing it for me?'

Chapter 23

Rohini wore a plain cotton sari and had a few changes of clothes in her college bag. At college she hurried through the last exam, didn't even check her answers.

At Churchgate, she walked up and down the platform, the same platform, where some months ago she'd broken up with Hanif. She looked over at the cold drinks kiosk and the bench where they had sat. An old man dozed on the bench now, his head hanging down to his chest, his mouth open. Her stomach was in knots as she paced. For the English exam she'd written: 'The alluring vision of the unknown . . . the counter-dream of holding on to the familiar.' She couldn't recall the context, but she uttered the words like a mantra. She stood on the platform as the train filled with passengers, a good three or four minutes.

Hanif appeared near the ticket counter, dressed in beige *churidar* and kurta. He waved and she felt herself gliding towards him. 'Ready,' he said, and she nodded. He suddenly wished he had told his parents of his plan to marry Rohini. They would be angry, and would have undoubtedly cautioned against it, but at least one set of parents would be in the know. Yesterday he had mulled over the idea of introducing them to Rohini, but in the end decided that he didn't want to risk anything going wrong at the last minute.

As they made their way to the taxi stand, he asked, 'Are you nervous?'

Rohini didn't know; more excited, than nervous, but it was something else as well. It was difficult to tell exactly. 'Do I look okay?' She adjusted the pleats of her sari.

'Beautiful,' he said.

Hanif instructed the driver, 'Bhindi Bazaar. Zakaria Masjid,' and they slid into the back seat, his small suitcase between them. The taxi smelled of sweat and *bidi* smoke. Wilting marigolds threaded together spilled from the ashtray in the center of the dashboard and next to the flowers a painted image of Hanuman. The taxi lurched into traffic and, as it circled Flora Fountain, Rohini stared at the stone edifice; rainwater in the carved tiered basins rushed in unruly streams to the great pool below. Down Hornsby Road, past *The Times of India* building, past the plump, silent figure of Queen Victoria, as they approached Crawford Market – her mother ordered mangoes from here during the hot season – she looked for the bird sellers who usually sat at the corner under the shade of the jacarandas. She smiled when she saw the mynahs, parrots, and doves flitting freely around the birdmen. The taxi turned left onto Muhammad Ali Road, the Muslim section of the city. Small shops – plumbers, cabinetmakers, and tailors – lined the miasmal lanes. Eateries advertised halal *kebabs* and chicken samosas. She looked up and saw laundry suspended from lines under open windows and imagined the families of the shopkeepers living in dark, dingy rooms upstairs. Down a lane choked with pedestrians, handcarts and bicycles, all heedless to the taxi's honking, but executing a subtle choreography that had them slipping out of the driver's path at the last moment. A small group of men gathered on the footpath; an ancient horse had collapsed and the owner was fanning it with a folded up newspaper. Women in black *burka*s crowded an *attar* shop called 'Cleopatra', its mirrored walls covered with miniature perfume bottles. Rohini wondered how she would ever walk the footpaths here, or buy anything in the shops. This was Bombay, but it seemed suddenly a foreign place.

'Do you know why this is called Bhindi Bazaar?' Hanif asked cheerfully.

'Why?' Rohini kept looking out the window. Her stomach churned. Was this a horrible mistake? She felt perspiration under her arms, at the back of her neck.

'It's not because *bhindi*s are sold there,' he said.

'Oh?' she said. She had never been to Bhindi Bazaar before.

'It's the area the British call "behind the bazaar",' Hanif grinned. 'You see?'

'No,' she said.

'The British said "behind the bazaar" and the Indians thought they said "bhindi bazaar".'

She giggled; it would all make sense in time. She turned to Hanif and took in his radiant face, the whimsical expression in his eyes. For a moment she felt elated, with a new confidence.

Hanif reached into the side pocket of his office bag. 'Here. For you.' He opened a small red velvet box. Inside, against white muslin lining and attached to a hook, lay a gold ring with tiny red rubies set in a simple flower pattern.

Rohini stared at the box and felt a flush of importance. She pictured him walking into a jewellery shop, the jeweller bringing out the rings from the glass cases for Hanif to examine. The ring from Jag with three rectangular diamonds and a halo of smaller diamonds around the circumference was considered exquisite; peering at it, her mother had beamed and nodded, 'It must be four or five carats at least!' But Rohini was certain Jag had not picked it himself.

Rohini looked about the taxi. 'I'll wear it later, after the ceremony,' she said to Hanif.

'Later I'll be a married man and I might forget,' he said. He closed the box and returned it to his office bag.

'I'll remind you, don't worry,' she teased, rolling her eyes at him.

As the taxi stopped in front of the mosque, Hanif reached for his wallet, and in the awkward movement of his hand, the tense set of his jaw, she sensed his nervousness. She wanted to say something to lighten his mood, but inside her, her own anxiety leapt to a new crescendo.

Pervez was standing near the entrance of the mosque, looking formal and smart in a white shirt with embroidery around the collar and cuffs. He held up a cloth bag and said he'd rented a camera. But he would wait outside; he had decided not to be involved in their foolhardy plan. 'You were supposed to be one of the witnesses,' Hanif said. Pervez shrugged and settled down on the front steps to wait. Rohini looked over her shoulder at him as she and Hanif entered the mosque.

The Imam, a middle-aged man with a greying beard, arranged for witnesses, two men in their mid-twenties, nephews, he said. Both wore white kurtas and fez-like caps. Rohini stood at the door of the sparse, windowless room that served as the cleric's office, her heart racing.

'You have brought money?' the Imam asked Hanif quietly. Hanif nodded as he adjusted the knot of the scarf covering his head. 'They will need something, too,' the Imam gestured towards his nephews. Hanif nodded to each of them.

A heavy-set woman appeared from a side door and led Rohini down a passageway to a latticed alcove where, turning on a tap, she directed Rohini to wash her arms and feet and face. The woman didn't offer a towel, and watched curiously as Rohini tried to brush off the water with her hands.

Rohini was led to another room and the Imam's voice was asking a question, and Hanif, after a nervous laugh, answered, 'Yes.' She saw the Imam opening a book, and then he was looking at her.

'Believe in the unity and oneness of God and that Mohammad is his Messenger,' the Imam stated. 'You may repeat after me,' he said, his face serene. 'There is no God but Allah and I bear witness that Mohammad is His Messenger.'

Rohini lowered her eyes. 'There is no God but Allah and I bear witness that Mohammad is His Messenger,' she said, her voice trembling but resolute. Ganesh, Krishna, Shiva, and Parvati ... the dozens of gods and goddesses she'd grown up with were wiped out of existence. She clamped her lips as her eyes darted about the floor.

They were in an antechamber of the main mosque. Except for a table pushed against a corner and two wooden benches near the doorway, the room was bare. A neatly rolled prayer carpet lay on one of the benches. Large windows stretching the length of the room opened onto a quiet courtyard. Most of the windows were closed because of the rainy season, but owing to the high ceilings the room was bright. Hanif stood a few steps behind Rohini, and next to him the Imam's nephews. All of them faced west, their backs to the windows. Framed verses from the Koran in Arabic calligraphy covered the wall in front of them.

'You must follow the Shahadah,' the Imam said. 'Practice the Five Pillars of Islam.' He opened the Koran and read some lines. Placing his right hand on the page, he looked up at Rohini and spoke in a slow, lilting voice: 'Have faith for Mohammad is your prophet. Pray five times a day facing,' he gestured westward with his right hand. 'Friday is the holy day and you must attend the mosque. Be charitable and give to the poor. During the month of Ramadan you must refrain from all food, even water, from sunrise to sunset. Finally, as a Muslim, you must go on pilgrimage, at least once, to Mecca.'

Rohini nodded. *Mohammad-Mecca-Mosque-Ramadan.* The words fell about her and she revelled in the newness.

'Your Muslim name,' the Imam said, 'with all respect and homage to Allah, the Almighty.' Taking a step forward he aligned himself to her left and read from the Koran. He came around to her right and said into her ear, 'Rezana. Rezana. Rezana.' She stood staring at the tiled floor. Rezana. It sounded light and airy, like delicate strands of a sweet confection. Behind her, she heard the two nephews shuffling, and Hanif . . . she glanced back quickly and saw the corners of his mouth break into a smile.

'Now we can proceed,' the Imam announced. He smoothed his beard, adjusted his vest, and shifted his feet. The room grew still. He tilted his head towards the ceiling, and recited a prayer rapidly. Then turning to Rohini, 'Are you happy and willing to marry this man?' He motioned for Hanif to move forward.

'Yes,' she said, without lifting her gaze.

'And you,' he asked Hanif. 'Are you happy and willing to marry this woman?'

'Yes,' Hanif said.

'You must promise to teach her the Koran. That is your duty.'

Hanif nodded. 'I promise.'

The Imam spoke of piety, mutual understanding, kindness, and social responsibility. At each breath he invoked the help and praise of Allah. Rohini listened attentively. The words sounded hypnotic and official.

> In the Name of Allah, Most Gracious, Most Merciful. Reverence your Lord, who created you from a single person, created, of like nature, his mate, and from them scattered seeds countless men and women . . .

> O you who believe! Fear Allah as he should be feared, and do not perish except in a state of Islam.

> Most Gracious, Most Merciful. Praise is to Allah, to Whom belong all things in the heavens and on earth . . .

Then, the affirmation.

'*Qabul*. Qabul. Qabul.' Hanif repeated the words, and looked at her indicating that she should do the same.

'Qabul-Qabul-Qabul,' she said, the words tumbling out of her in one breath. Her gaze left the floor and settled on Hanif's face – she saw his lips moving, still saying, 'Qabul, qabul,' to himself.

She focused on the Arabic calligraphy on the wall, at the maze of loops, dots, lines, and dashes as the Imam began talking about the Hadith, the teachings of the Prophet

Mohammad. From a table near the wall, the Imam brought out what Hanif later told her was the *Nikkah-nama*. Printed on heavy parchment paper, the main text ran almost the length of the page. The Imam gestured for them to come closer to the table. She watched the Imam dip the pen in the pot of black ink. Holding his beard back with one hand and, with the tip of his tongue sticking out in concentration, he put the date on the document, August 14, 1947. He signed on the first line at the bottom, *Imam Khalid Ali Abdullah Akhtar*. There was artistry to the Imam's signature and she thought the calligraphy in the frames on the wall might be in his hand.

Under the Imam's name, Hanif signed, *Hanif Wali Hussein*, the second 'H' larger and bolder than the other letters, as he re-dipped the pen in ink.

Clutching the pen, she hesitated. Was she Rohini or Rezana?

The Imam seemed to have read her mind. 'Rezana,' he said, matter-of-factly.

With an unusually steady hand, she wrote, *Rezana Hussein*. She stared at the words and understood the finality of her decision, the nagging barrage of doubts willfully laid to rest.

The two nephews stepped forward and added their names as witnesses to the document.

The Imam reached for a small bowl on the table and uncovered the voile cloth. 'Keep the documents safely,' he instructed Rohini, while he offered her the bowl of dates. 'You will need the papers to enter the holy cities.'

She looked up at the Imam and nodded. His eyes were round and watery and the expression in them kind, as though he understood what she had left behind.

When Hanif and Rohini emerged from the mosque, it had started to drizzle. Pervez, standing under an awning, ran towards them. 'Did you . . .?'

Hanif said, 'Her new name is Rezana!'

'Rezana?' Pervez said, scanning her face for signs of any mystical transformation.

She smiled uneasily.

'Rezana. A nice Muslim name,' Pervez said. 'From now on I will call you Rezana-*begum*.' He bowed in mock seriousness before her. 'Okay,' he said, jovially, 'time for a photo.' He directed them under the awning and as they got into position, side-by-side, Pervez reached over and put Hanif's hand around Rohini's shoulder. 'You must *act* married now.'

Pervez stepped back, bent his knees a little, aimed the rented camera and clicked.

'Now, let's go to Gaylord!' Pervez suggested.

Hanif hesitated.

'It's a special occasion,' Pervez insisted.

The restaurant was practically empty; it was much too early for the dinner crowd. Hanif glanced at the vacant piano, the drums, and the black instrument cases. He imagined men in dark suits, ladies in saris or long dresses, dancing to Western music. He looked at Rohini beside him – oh, but she was Rezana now, he reminded himself happily. *Rezana, Rezana* – he tried out her new name.

A starched waiter seated them at a table near the window. Outside, afternoon was ceding to evening. The city seemed quiet, as though holding its breath, waiting for the stroke of midnight when the green, white and orange Indian flag would replace the red, white and blue of the British Union.

Hanif stroked the gold 'G' insignia embossed on the fine white plate and ran his fingers over the shiny silverware.

'Slightly better than Café Royal, don't you think?' Pervez asked with a grin.

They ordered finger sandwiches and tea. 'And we'll take cake afterwards,' Hanif announced to the waiter as he closed the leather-bound menu.

While they waited for the food, Hanif gave Pervez a white envelope. 'Can you please deliver this to Sagar Mahal?'

'What is it?' Pervez picked up the envelope and held it to the light.

'A letter. I've explained everything.'

'What? Me? You want *me* to deliver this!' Pervez put the envelope back on the table and shook his head. 'No, Hanif. I'm sorry.'

Rohini looked at the envelope with curiosity and terror.

Hanif nodded at her, then glared at Pervez. 'Who else will deliver it?'

'Send it by post,' Pervez said, fidgeting with his fork.

'Post?' Hanif said, irritated. 'Her people will be worried. It should be delivered tonight. Are you scared to be our messenger, or what?'

Rohini looked at Pervez and, recalling his plans to gather weapons and head an insurgency, nudged the envelope towards him.

When the waiter returned with the sandwiches and tea, they ate in silence. The slices of cake, which were speckled with almonds, came with a swirl of chocolate cream and a triangular wafer, but the celebratory mood had vanished from the table. After Hanif paid the bill and they got up to leave, Pervez slipped the envelope in his shirt pocket. 'Thanks,' Hanif said. 'I owe you a favour.'

'You owe me many favours,' Pervez said, grimly.

Outside, Hanif and Rezana got into a taxi; Pervez said he would walk to the station.

'Good luck,' Pervez shouted as the taxi pulled away.

They were silent in the taxi. An evening sky spotted with billowy clouds and occasional bursts of crimson stretched over the city. The roads were empty and they reached Colaba within minutes.

ನ೪

Hotel Peacock was a three-storey building on a tree-lined lane. One side of the hotel overlooked the harbour, and the other faced a row of shops. Graffiti and posters covered the compound wall. There was no driveway leading to the door, only an irregular stone path with patches of grass and pebbles on either side. Flowering bushes and vines grew randomly around the building. In one corner insects flitted over the green water of a small pond and a weathered life-size figurine of a boy with a fishing rod stood at the edge.

At the reception desk, Mr Kumar, a middle-aged man with a wide, receding forehead was expecting them. He wore a suit, the jacket much too big for him, and a bow tie. 'I forgot to ask your address when you phoned, sir. Mr and Mrs Hanif Hussein. Please sir, be kind enough to enter your home address in my book.' He opened the guest register and flipped to a clean page. 'Have you ever been to Delhi, sir?'

As Hanif wrote in the register, Mr Kumar kept chatting.

'Look for her? Where?' Motilal plucked a leaf from the jasmine vine, tore it in bits and flung the fragments over the unruly plant.

Harshaba threw her arms up in the air. Sinking into a chair she put her head in her hands.

Mahesh, Sumitra and Amrita, emerged from the divankhana, their faces covered in worry. And behind them, Shrikant and Prema.

'We should go to the police station,' Mahesh said.

'Yes,' Shrikant said, 'There are riots because of Independence. We should inform the police, in case she has been caught in the trouble.'

'Police?' Harshaba shot up from the chair, her eyes darting to the clock, then to the gates.

Motilal and Mahesh set off in the car with Vincent. The road to the police station was desolate, but Motilal kept scanning the footpaths as they rounded the corner near the public gardens and the dairy stand. 'You look on that side,' he said to Mahesh. Past the post office the footpath ended and there was only the stretch of swamp and patches of quicksand on either side of the two-lane road until they reached Andheri.

The police station was closed, its doors bolted and padlocked.

'Drive to the college,' Motilal said to Vincent as they got back into the car.

Vincent kept talking to himself about Rohini and the blessed Mother Mary, pressing the accelerator and letting up. Motilal clutched the armrest with one hand, and gripped the seat in front with the other. 'Drive slowly,' he said to Vincent. 'Were you drinking tonight?'

'Ah, Delhi. *Best* city in the world,' Mr. Kumar smiled. 'My uncle lives there. He's getting old, but he's the *best* uncle in the world. Runs a hotel near Connaught Place. Also called Hotel Peacock. *Best* hotel in the world. If you ever go to Delhi, sir, please stay at Hotel Peacock. So much to see in our nation's capital – Humayun's Tomb, Qutab Minar, Shalimar Gardens, Red Fort, Chandni Chowk. Ah, Chandni Chowk – *best* tandoori chicken in the world,' he smacked his lips. 'But I've never been to Agra. We should open a hotel in Agra, I keep telling my uncle. All foreign tourists go there to see Taj Mahal, *best* Taj Mahal in the world. And your business, sir?'

'Radio. All India Radio,' Hanif said.

'Ah, radio,' Mr Kumar beamed. 'What do you do? Sports? Cricket? Ah, yes, cricket, *best* sport in the world. You do cricket commentary?'

'Music,' Hanif said.

'Oh . . .' Mr Kumar looked disappointed. He surveyed the room keys that dangled from brass peacock rings on a board behind him. 'Let me see. Two-zero-five has a radio,' he said with renewed enthusiasm. 'And attached bath. *Best* room in the world.' He removed the peacock key and handed it to Hanif. 'Will you be taking bed tea in the morning or coming down to the verandah? Madam,' he bowed to Rezana, 'allow me to show you the verandah. *Best* verandah in the world.'

Mr Kumar led them down a hallway beyond the reception desk through a beaded curtain to a verandah with tables and chairs. A roof of corrugated-iron sheets covered the area, but still the rain had leaked through and left puddles of blackish water.

'Yes, yes, it's fine. We'll be down in the morning,' Hanif said hurriedly, eager to get away from Mr Kumar. The *best* Mr Kumar in the world, he thought to himself.

Upstairs, the best room in the world had a peacock-patterned coverlet on the bed. A vinyl sofa was pushed to a corner, and beaded curtains, similar to the ones downstairs, hung between the sofa and the bed. A radio sat ceremoniously on a shelf, its thick black wire stretching across the wall to a plug. 'There's a balcony,' Hanif said to Rezana, opening the glass door. 'Come, see the view.' It was two steps down into the balcony. He turned and held out his hand to help her.

Chapter 24

At Sagar Mahal, a balmy breeze brushed the branches the palms and stirred the birds that perched quiet amon the bamboo. Motilal paced the front verandah, thirty step to the right, and thirty to the left. Mosquitoes spiralled and looped around the dusty light bulbs. A mild scent of jasmine permeated the air. Ordinarily the night chowkidar would have locked the gates by this time, but he, too, while puffing on a beedi, wandered outside and looked up the dark, deserted road.

'Was there a music programme at college?' Motilal asked Harshaba, even though he knew the answer. With his hands clasped behind his back, head and shoulders stooped forward, he continued pacing.

'What programme? It was the last day of exams.' Harshaba squinted at the clock that hung above the door to the kitchen. 'Something has happened. Maybe we should telephone Dr Kapoor.'

'Dr Kapoor? What will he do? Is anyone sick?'

The sound of a car in the distance arrested Harshaba's attention, but the headlights flared and faded.

'Why don't you take the car with Vincent and go look for her?' she said. 'I hope that idiot driver hasn't been drinking tonight.'

'Ah, Delhi. *Best* city in the world,' Mr. Kumar smiled. 'My uncle lives there. He's getting old, but he's the *best* uncle in the world. Runs a hotel near Connaught Place. Also called Hotel Peacock. *Best* hotel in the world. If you ever go to Delhi, sir, please stay at Hotel Peacock. So much to see in our nation's capital – Humayun's Tomb, Qutab Minar, Shalimar Gardens, Red Fort, Chandni Chowk. Ah, Chandni Chowk – *best* tandoori chicken in the world,' he smacked his lips. 'But I've never been to Agra. We should open a hotel in Agra, I keep telling my uncle. All foreign tourists go there to see Taj Mahal, *best* Taj Mahal in the world. And your business, sir?'

'Radio. All India Radio,' Hanif said.

'Ah, radio,' Mr Kumar beamed. 'What do you do? Sports? Cricket? Ah, yes, cricket, *best* sport in the world. You do cricket commentary?'

'Music,' Hanif said.

'Oh . . .' Mr Kumar looked disappointed. He surveyed the room keys that dangled from brass peacock rings on a board behind him. 'Let me see. Two-zero-five has a radio,' he said with renewed enthusiasm. 'And attached bath. *Best* room in the world.' He removed the peacock key and handed it to Hanif. 'Will you be taking bed tea in the morning or coming down to the verandah? Madam,' he bowed to Rezana, 'allow me to show you the verandah. *Best* verandah in the world.'

Mr Kumar led them down a hallway beyond the reception desk through a beaded curtain to a verandah with tables and chairs. A roof of corrugated-iron sheets covered the area, but still the rain had leaked through and left puddles of blackish water.

'Yes, yes, it's fine. We'll be down in the morning,' Hanif said hurriedly, eager to get away from Mr Kumar. The *best* Mr Kumar in the world, he thought to himself.

Upstairs, the best room in the world had a peacock-patterned coverlet on the bed. A vinyl sofa was pushed to a corner, and beaded curtains, similar to the ones downstairs, hung between the sofa and the bed. A radio sat ceremoniously on a shelf, its thick black wire stretching across the wall to a plug. 'There's a balcony,' Hanif said to Rezana, opening the glass door. 'Come, see the view.' It was two steps down into the balcony. He turned and held out his hand to help her.

Chapter 24

At Sagar Mahal, a balmy breeze brushed the branches of the palms and stirred the birds that perched quiet among the bamboo. Motilal paced the front verandah, thirty steps to the right, and thirty to the left. Mosquitoes spiralled and looped around the dusty light bulbs. A mild scent of jasmine permeated the air. Ordinarily the night chowkidar would have locked the gates by this time, but he, too, while puffing on a beedi, wandered outside and looked up the dark, deserted road.

'Was there a music programme at college?' Motilal asked Harshaba, even though he knew the answer. With his hands clasped behind his back, head and shoulders stooped forward, he continued pacing.

'What programme? It was the last day of exams.' Harshaba squinted at the clock that hung above the door to the kitchen. 'Something has happened. Maybe we should telephone Dr Kapoor.'

'Dr Kapoor? What will he do? Is anyone sick?'

The sound of a car in the distance arrested Harshaba's attention, but the headlights flared and faded.

'Why don't you take the car with Vincent and go look for her?' she said. 'I hope that idiot driver hasn't been drinking tonight.'

'Look for her? Where?' Motilal plucked a leaf from the jasmine vine, tore it in bits and flung the fragments over the unruly plant.

Harshaba threw her arms up in the air. Sinking into a chair she put her head in her hands.

Mahesh, Sumitra and Amrita, emerged from the divankhana, their faces covered in worry. And behind them, Shrikant and Prema.

'We should go to the police station,' Mahesh said.

'Yes,' Shrikant said, 'There are riots because of Independence. We should inform the police, in case she has been caught in the trouble.'

'Police?' Harshaba shot up from the chair, her eyes darting to the clock, then to the gates.

Motilal and Mahesh set off in the car with Vincent. The road to the police station was desolate, but Motilal kept scanning the footpaths as they rounded the corner near the public gardens and the dairy stand. 'You look on that side,' he said to Mahesh. Past the post office the footpath ended and there was only the stretch of swamp and patches of quicksand on either side of the two-lane road until they reached Andheri.

The police station was closed, its doors bolted and padlocked.

'Drive to the college,' Motilal said to Vincent as they got back into the car.

Vincent kept talking to himself about Rohini and the blessed Mother Mary, pressing the accelerator and letting up. Motilal clutched the armrest with one hand, and gripped the seat in front with the other. 'Drive slowly,' he said to Vincent. 'Were you drinking tonight?'